MORTAL CHAOS
SPEED FREAKS

Also by Matt Dickinson

Mortal Chaos
Deep Oblivion

1

CYPRESS FOREST, HIDA MOUNTAIN RANGE, JAPAN

08:54 a.m. Local time

The butterfly was an Alpine Grayling, a two-day-old creature living in a clearing in a valley of the Hida mountain range in Japan.

This particular butterfly was a male, one of a late brood, hatching in the final moments of autumn warmth, and programmed by nature to feed, locate a female, and mate—all in a ten day lifespan before the first chill nights of the coming winter would end the struggle for life.

Male butterflies are frequently territorial, they chase competitors away with a rising 'dance' that to an uneducated observer can look like a mating ritual.

The butterfly was dancing now, sparring with a rival which soon gave up the challenge and flew away into the forest. The Alpine Grayling descended to ground level and flitted among the wild flowers, feeding on the nectar with its long proboscis as bees and beetles jostled for space.

Then it sensed a threat; danger was in the air.

2

CYPRESS FOREST, HIDA MOUNTAIN RANGE, JAPAN

The butterfly collector was Professor Daichi Yamada, an entomologist from the Institute of Insect Systemization and Ecology in Osaka.

He was midway through his annual field trip, based in a tent way off the beaten track.

Yamada had set out alone at seven a.m. with his net and collecting boxes. He was a fit man for a sixty year old: tramping around these rugged mountains was a routine working day for this white-haired academic even if he often got lost along the way.

Now he was deep in a forested zone of cypress trees, searching for specimens which were missing from his collection.

He reached a clearing filled with flowers. Suddenly he saw it. An Alpine Grayling, a healthy looking specimen which had been on his hit list for a while. The brown-coloured butterfly was darting around nervously, seeming to sense a hint of danger.

Yamada crept forward on his hands and knees. Midges and biting flies were buzzing around his ears and neck but their irritating stings were the last thing on his mind at that moment.

He held out the collecting net, stretching to the limit as the butterfly came tantalizingly close.

3

At that exact moment, halfway round the world, in the sweltering heat of a Rio night, a thirteen-year-old boy was struggling to get a huge load of rubbish onto his back. It was a couple of hours before midnight local time, an hour when more fortunate children would be safely tucked up in bed.

The kid was slight of frame, malnourished, in fact, with the watchful, prematurely adult eyes of a boy who suspects his life is worthless and who has seen too much cruelty at too young an age. His real name was Remo, but the people of the *favela*—the shanty town—called him the 'pig-boy'.

The reason for the nickname was simple: Remo was one of the pigswill porters for the township, spending his time searching for rotting vegetables and other organic waste behind supermarkets and market stalls, then selling it for a pittance by the containerful to people who kept pigs in their gardens and yards.

The work was intensely physical and on occasions it was also downright dangerous; shopkeepers in the smarter parts of town didn't want the tone of their establishments lowered by kids like the 'pig-boy' rooting in their bins.

Sometimes they would set their guard dogs on him, just for fun. Remo had the scars on his calves to prove it.

4

The professor lunged forward, swiping the collecting net in a wild arc.

Missed. The Alpine Grayling dodged the mesh with a sudden swerve to the right.

The professor mopped sweat away from his eyes. He could have let it go but that wasn't Yamada's style. He was a doggedly determined man, and that specimen was one he had been searching for for several years.

The butterfly led the academic far from the clearing, into a zone of chest-high poplar bushes.

Yamada pushed his way into the dense thicket.

The butterfly descended. Nearly within reach. The professor jumped up, the mesh of his collecting net making a swishing noise in the air as he came within an ace of catching it.

Then he almost jumped out of his skin.

A black bear was sleeping right there in the thicket.

And the professor had just blundered into it.

He froze. But it was already too late.

The bear was awake. And it was mad as hell.

The creature bellowed out a mighty cry, long strings of drool dripping from a mouth filled with razor-sharp teeth.

5

Back in Rio, a souped-up Hummer jeep was racing through the streets of the *favela*, thrash metal blasting on the stereo. The chunky vehicle was almost too big to squeeze through the alleys of the slum, the shanty buildings zooming past in a crazy flash of speed as the driver whooped and laughed with drunken pleasure.

A fifteen-year-old driver with no licence and a belly full of rum.

The vehicle was a real piece of work, a blinged-up bullet-proof monster which had cost more than two hundred thousand dollars. It was sprayed in gold, quartz pimp-lights studded into the alloys, smoked-glass windows protecting the occupants from curious eyes.

The owner of this travelling fortress was a man as dangerous as he was rich. Leonardo was one of Rio's more notorious drug barons, a cunning backstreet mobster who had got lucky and pulled off some huge deals. Now, thanks to a series of violent coups against his rivals he was king of the *favela*, a much feared gangster with a small army of enforcers and dealers working for him.

The driver—Leonardo's son Casio—was following enthusiastically in his father's dubious footsteps. He even mimicked Leonardo's look, with intricate buzz-cut hairstyle and razor-striped brows.

'Don't be such a wimp!' Leonardo goaded his son. 'I don't want to see that speedo fall below sixty.'

5

Leonardo twisted the cap off a bottle of whisky and swigged hard on the liquor as Casio pushed the Hummer even harder down the dirty alleys. 'You're doing good,' Leonardo said, 'I'm proud of you, son.'

6

CYPRESS FOREST, HIDA MOUNTAIN RANGE, JAPAN

The bear pawed the ground, ripping up roots and clouds of earth with powerful claws. The professor stood stock still, quivering with terror, his mind racing through half-remembered tips on how to survive a bear encounter.

The truth is this: if you are going to bump into a bear in the wilderness of Japan (or in any wilderness for that matter), it really is advisable *not* to meet one in the autumn.

At that time of the year bears become anxious. They sense that winter is coming and it makes them nervous. They are painfully aware that they have to build up crucial body fat to survive the long hibernation. They get stressed, inclined to pick a fight. Just a year or so earlier a bad-tempered black bear had seriously injured nine people in a small mountain town nearby.

It just wandered out of the woods and mauled them for no reason whatsoever other than it was having a bad day.

This bear was having a bad day as well.

And the hapless professor had just made it worse.

Seconds later, the creature charged.

7

At that instant in Tokyo, two hundred miles to the east, a fourteen-year-old girl called Saki arrived at the central railway station and boarded a bullet train for Nagano.

Saki was getting some curious looks from her fellow passengers.

It's not every day you see a pet rat on a train.

The rat was a two-year-old creature, sitting now on Saki's lap in its little cage. Its name was 'Brad': Japanese girls are crazy about Mr Pitt.

Saki spent quite a bit of time on the bullet train: her parents had split up a year before, forcing her to shuttle backwards and forwards between her mother in Tokyo and her father in Nagano. Since then she had felt as if her life was sliced in two—with neither half complete.

No wonder Brad the rat had become so important to her. At least he was company on the endless journeys from one parent to another.

Plus, secretly, Saki liked the way he freaked people out.

Saki was feeling thirsty. She needed a soda. She picked up the little cage by its carrying handle and set off towards the catering car. As she did so she heard the doors shut with a gentle hiss.

The bullet train pulled out of the station and began to pick up speed.

8

8

CYPRESS FOREST, HIDA MOUNTAIN RANGE, JAPAN

Yamada crashed through the thicket, the galloping bear rapidly gaining on him. It was phenomenally fast for such a huge creature.

Control the panic. Don't lose control.

Even as he ran, the professor was thinking what to do. Should he lie on the floor and play dead? Try to climb a tree? Keep running in the hope he could outpace the bear?

He decided to throw his rucksack.

Perhaps the bear would be distracted by it. Attack the rucksack instead of him?

He shrugged off the straps and slung the bag into the undergrowth as he ran. But the creature ignored it and kept coming. The professor risked a glance back. The bear was just a few metres behind him and it certainly didn't look as if it was going to give up the chase.

One thing was sure. This was no bluff charge. The creature was going to teach this blundering human a lesson he would not forget.

The professor saw a cypress tree ahead. It had a low hanging bough which he might just reach if he jumped. He leapt for the branch, curling both hands around it . . .

9

The Hummer blitzed a trail through the slum, the two-tone horn blaring, sending roosting chickens squawking into the night. A couple of late-night revellers dived for a ditch as the vehicle roared past. Leonardo zapped down the window and fired his pistol into the sky, the ripe stench of rotting rubbish filling his nostrils as he breathed in the night air.

'Wake up, losers!' Leonardo screamed. 'There's no time to sleep!'

Casio slammed the Hummer into top gear, a big grin splitting his young face. It was shaping up into a great night.

Just an hour or so earlier, Casio and his thuggish mates had been downtown, targeting a family of rich American tourists eating at one of Rio's late-night food malls. There were two young boys with the family, both laden with attractive gadgets and innocent as new-born lambs.

Casio and his gang had waited until the two boys went to the rest room, cornered them there, slapped them around a bit and mugged them of their toys.

The thugs had split the spoils; Casio—the ringleader— coming out of it with the American kids' iPhone and a state-of-the-art MP4 player.

The look of raw fear on the kids' faces had been a buzz. Sure, they were only eleven or twelve years old, but it still made Casio feel like a real gangster.

He loved that rush. There was nothing like it.

10

CYPRESS FOREST, HIDA MOUNTAIN RANGE, JAPAN

Professor Yamada made it to the main trunk and scrambled awkwardly up to the highest point of the tree. He was shaking with morbid fear as he watched the angry bear pace backwards and forwards on the grass beneath him.

Would it try and climb the tree?

If it did he had no idea what he would do.

He forced himself to get his brain in check. A call. He had to get some help. Fast. He needed someone to come and shoot that bear before it killed him.

Yamada took out his mobile and dialled the emergency services.

'Hello. What is the nature of your emergency?'

'M . . . m . . . m . . . m . . . my . . . n . . . n . . . n—'

Yamada could have wept with frustration. He had suffered from neurogenic stuttering ever since childhood and—now of all moments—the stress of the bear incident had brought on an attack.

'Speak up please, caller. I am not hearing you properly.'

'N . . . n . . . n . . . n . . . n . . . name . . .'

The police operative did her best but she could not understand a single word that the professor said.

Yamada terminated the call. The bear was still staring up at him with furious intent. Then he remembered a colleague; a friend who could understand him well even when his stuttering attacks were at their worst.

Yamada selected his contacts folder.

11

Remo the 'pig-boy' turned down a sewage-filled alley and found the bins of a fast-food restaurant. Years working in the dark had given him phenomenal night vision. He was using the faint glimmer of starlight to help him sift through the waste.

There was plenty of good food there for pigs: half-eaten pizza crusts, rock-hard rinds of mouldy cheese, withered old potatoes which were soggy to the touch.

Remo got to work. Filling up his sack.

As he worked he thought about his mother, lying sick in a tumbledown hut on the other side of town. Her working days as a factory cleaner were over; her lungs riddled with disease. Remo's father Carlito was no longer around; he'd gone to sea on an oil tanker two years earlier and they'd never heard a word since.

There was no safety net for the inhabitants of the *favela*. No sickness benefit. No government support. Neighbours could be kind, but how often can you ask for help from people who have themselves got nothing?

That was why Remo had started up the waste collecting. Without the few coins he brought home to his mother every Sunday she would starve to death. That was the hard reality of life in the *favela*.

Remo longed to leave the stinking little tin shack where he lived. Sometimes he fantasized about taking his mother back to the sugar cane plantation where she had spent her childhood. The stories she told about that place . . . it seemed like a sweet heaven: clean sheets, hot food . . .

A scabby dog growled at him from the shadows.

Dream on, he thought. *Get real.* This is how it's always going to be.

12

SHINKANSEN BULLET TRAIN, EN-ROUTE NAGANO, JAPAN

The recipient of the professor's call was Dr Roger Stansfield, and at that moment he was sitting with a coffee in seat 11b in car number two of the Nagano-bound bullet train.

Stansfield was one of Yamada's closest colleagues, a native of Dublin in Ireland who had married a Japanese girl many years ago, learned the language, and settled into academic life as a biologist.

Stansfield gave a little sigh as he saw who was calling him. He had a soft spot for the old academic even if the professor was scatterbrained to the point of distraction.

'R . . . r . . . r . . . r . . . Roger.' Yamada's stutter was as bad as Stansfield had ever heard it and he knew immediately that the prof had to be totally stressed out. 'I'm . . . (pause) a t . . . t . . . t . . . t-t-t-tree . . . (pause) a b . . . b . . . b . . . bear . . . (pause) . . . help.'

The line was a bad one and Stansfield was fighting to decipher the message. 'What? I can't hear you. Did you say something about a . . . *bear*?'

Then the call went dead.

Stansfield frowned as he thought this through. The call had been mystifying to say the least. Did Yamada say 'bear' . . . and 'tree'?

The academic decided he would call Yamada back, but he didn't want to make the call from his seat where the conversation would excite interest from his fellow travellers.

He rose abruptly from his seat but he forgot about the coffee sitting on the small table in front of him.

The drink went flying into the aisle.

13

NELSON MUSTER'S FLAT, SEATTLE, USA

Seven thousand seven hundred kilometres to the east—in Seattle on the west coast of the USA—a twenty year old by the name of Nelson F. Muster waddled into his computer den. It was a few minutes after five p.m. local time and he had been awake for about ten minutes.

Nelson was a trainspotter. An international trainspotter as he grandly called himself. Not that he had ever been out of his home town.

If he had been born a decade or two earlier, Nelson would have spent most of his waking hours sitting on a windswept platform on a busy trunk line, scribbling numbers in a notebook with a pencil stub as locomotives chundered past.

At least then he might have had to speak to someone face to face. A bit of real live human interaction might have come into his life.

But no. Nelson's world was lived online, courtesy of the webcams which had been installed in many of the world's most important railway stations.

Clicking from one webcam site to another, he could span the globe at a click of his mouse, moving from one live station webcam to another as he pleased. Simultaneously, he could watch the Trans-Siberian express pull out of the station at Irkutsk, and still keep an eye on the commuter trains zapping in and out of New York.

Station webcams had opened up a whole universe of possibility to Nelson.

They truly made him happy.

14

SHINKANSEN BULLET TRAIN, EN-ROUTE NAGANO, JAPAN

Saki was walking down the aisle of car number two, heading for the catering car, when the anxious looking man with the mobile suddenly shot up from his seat.

His styrofoam cup of coffee tipped, then fell into the aisle . . . and right over the carrying cage containing Saki's pet rat.

The rat jumped back in shock as the scalding liquid hit its back.

Saki unclipped the catch and opened the little door to the cage. She reached in for the rat and took it firmly in her hand. The little rodent was scared half to death, hissing with fear as the pain of the scalding coffee overwhelmed it. Saki took off her scarf, dabbed at the rat's fur to try to remove the liquid.

'OK my little one.' She tried to soothe the rat with a few calming words.

Then it happened.

Brad the rat bit Saki on the thumb. He'd never done that before.

'Ow!' Saki pulled her hand back fast in a reflex reaction.

The rat dropped to the floor and ran down the central aisle of the wagon.

15

Nelson was just about to click on the first station webcam of the day when the telephone rang. He sighed when he saw his mother's number on the ID screen, guessing immediately what she was calling about.

'Did you take your medication?' she asked. 'You know what happens when you don't.'

Nelson groaned. *Nag nag nag.* He hated taking those darn pills but since he'd been diagnosed with Intermittent Explosive Disorder he'd had to buckle down and swallow them on a daily basis.

Even he had to admit that they had calmed him down a lot.

'OK, OK! I'll go and get them now,' he promised.

Nelson put down the receiver and went to the bathroom cabinet. He found the three bottles and selected one tablet from each:

Lithium: a mood stabilizer. Propanolol: a regulator of blood pressure and anxiety. And Tegretol to prevent seizures.

Taken together, these three drugs had brought Nelson's IED under control. No more explosions of violence and aggression. No more impulsive rages which were totally out of proportion to the provoking incident. He could function as a normal member of society.

So long as he took the drugs.

Nelson returned to his computer den and placed the three little tablets on the desk.

I'll take them in a minute, he thought.

16

Brad the rat scampered down the central aisle of the Shinkansen carriage. It was spotted almost immediately by several passengers.

'A rat!'

Straight away, the screaming and commotion began. The rat ran across someone's foot. Children gasped excitedly as they saw the lithe little beast darting to and fro.

A huge German man sitting in seat 34a had an umbrella with him. He had little fear of rats and he loathed them with a vengeance. He got up from his seat and followed the rat down to the end of the wagon.

The rat was cornered. Stress levels were soaring as it was surrounded by people. It tried to dart through someone's legs then retreated as the German man with the umbrella slammed the weapon down just centimetres from the creature's head.

Just a few seats away, a couple of American backpackers were watching the rampaging rat incident with unrestrained delight. They were Sam and Cody, both nineteen, and there was nothing they liked more than a bit of mayhem to liven up a dull journey.

'Shoot it on your iPhone,' Sam urged Cody. 'Quickly!'

Cody whipped out his iPhone and clicked it rapidly onto video mode. He framed up on the action as the rat scooted back and forth around the carriage, the screams of the passengers driving it crazy.

The florid-looking German man advanced on the creature, umbrella raised threateningly. Cody was filming the whole thing, laughing fit to bust at the same time.

17

As the rat fiasco unfolded, another drama was evolving some distance ahead of the bullet train's position. Two thrillseeking local boys were breaking into the freight yard at Kariuzawa railway station on a secret and potentially dangerous mission.

The previous night, at three o'clock in the morning, they had cut a section of the security fence away with a pair of wire cutters.

Now the bullet train was speeding towards them.

The boys were Takumi and Riku, adrenaline sports fans and avid watchers of reality stunt shows which pushed the limits. Every spare moment was spent scanning the archives of YouTube for the latest viral video featuring extreme skateboarders and surfers—and the crazier the stunt the more they liked it.

Recently they had heard a story about a sixteen-year-old kid from Nagano who—so the legend went—had surfed the bullet train at two hundred and fifty kilometres an hour. Standing on the roof. No one knew if it was real or not but it sounded exceptionally cool.

Takumi and Riku were in love with the idea. How would that feel? Standing in the surfing stance as the countryside rushed past at that insane speed?

Was it even possible? Maybe the wind speed would knock them off their feet. They really had no idea.

From that moment these two fifteen-year-old boys were fixated on one mission.

Surf a bullet train. Film it on a mobile.

Put it on YouTube, and become legends themselves.

18

Roger Stansfield watched the outraged passengers with a stinging sense of shame. Spilling that coffee over the girl's pet had been stupid. But the need to call the professor back was pressing; he selected recall.

'So. What's the problem, professor?'

The connection was better this time. Also, Yamada's stress-related stutter had eased a bit and—by concentrating hard—Stansfield was able to understand him. The academic listened in horror as he heard Yamada's explanation of the bear attack.

'What is the bear doing now?'

'W . . . w . . . w . . . waiting here. I n-n-need you to call the p . . . p . . . p-police.'

'But where are you exactly?' Stansfield asked his colleague. 'If I call the rescue authorities they're going to need a grid reference. Have you got a GPS with you?'

'No. But I'm in the mountains . . . two days w . . . w . . . w-walk from Nagano. And I can see a lake. And a r . . . r . . . r-railway track.'

'Now we're getting somewhere,' Stansfield told him. 'Are you north, south, east, or west of the lake?'

'Ermm. W . . . w . . . w-west. No, s . . . s-s-s-south. Maybe.'

Hopeless, Stansfield thought, absolutely hopeless. The prof evidently didn't have a clue where he was.

'OK. Sit tight. I'm going to get things rolling for you.'

Stansfield terminated the call and called the police. He would have to relay them the information as best he could and hope that a rescue team would get lucky and find Yamada.

19

Occasionally, Nelson's mother would try and get him interested in something else: reading, for example. Jigsaws. Birdwatching. Anything but sitting in front of those screens.

She might as well not have bothered; Nelson was as addicted to railway station webcams as he was to Twinkies and jelly beans.

'I live in a virtual world,' he would tell his mother when she beseeched him to get out of his chair—at least to have a shower. 'It's a world that you cannot possibly understand.'

Nelson's mother had never so much as sent an email in her life.

The fact that she had to work ten hour shifts cleaning out the wards at a psychiatric hospital to keep her tech-addicted son updated with the latest expensive Mac . . . the fastest broadband connection . . . the latest webcam technology . . . etc., etc., etc., was of little or no concern to this supremely selfish individual.

Who still hadn't taken his pills and who now decided it was time for his first coffee of the day.

He waddled to the kitchen and got to work. Nelson liked his coffee real: freshly ground Colombian beans and the type of Italian coffee maker that sits on the flame so that the boiling water bubbles up through the grounds.

He clicked on the gas, heard the flare as it ignited.

He put the coffee pot in place then padded back to his webcams.

20

The German went into the attack. Cody stood so he could get a better shot on his video.

The sharp end of the umbrella jabbed hard. The rat leapt up, fangs bared, jumping for its life with a shrill squeal of terror. The umbrella tip grazed the creature's belly. It was a small wound—not lethal—but the small rat was bleeding now and desperate for escape.

'Let me through!' Saki cried. 'He's my pet!'

'I hope you're getting this, dude,' Sam snorted through his tears of delight.

'Every frame!' Cody's only problem was keeping the camera steady he was laughing so much.

Then everything kicked off into true farce.

Brad the rat dashed for the only dark sanctuary he could see: the flapping interior of the German man's corduroy trousers.

'My God! He's gone up! He's gone up!' the German man screamed.

Brad the rat squirmed up the inside of the trouser leg, the tourist beating at the moving bulge with desperate blows of his fists. Cody was getting *all* the action as the man's screams got higher pitched and more hysterical.

Suddenly the tourist doubled up. 'He's bitten it! He's bitten it, by God!' The rat shot down the other trouser leg and emerged into the daylight. The electric door suddenly opened. Primitive instincts took over as the rat saw the opportunity.

The creature scuttled out of the wagon into the catering car and headed for cover.

21

The helicopter was a Eurocopter EC135. It was sitting on the helipad at the Nagano Prefecture Mountain Rescue Unit headquarters when the emergency call came in.

The EC135 is a world class performer as a search and rescue helicopter. It has a powerful twin engine power plant using two Pratt and Whitney Canada PW206B2s rated at 419kW continuous power output—more than enough juice to enable the machine to operate effectively at high altitude in the Hida mountain range.

The three-man rescue team were quick to respond; it took them less than two minutes to scramble from the mess room to the aircraft.

The co-pilot took the controls as the engines kicked in and the rotors began to turn. He did a final visual check of the surroundings, changing the pitch on the main rotors as he twisted the throttle to find more power.

The EC135 hovered a couple of metres in the air for approximately forty-five seconds as the crew ran through the final cockpit checks.

Then the pilot pushed the cyclic control stick forward, lowering the nose so that the aircraft moved forward as he increased the power yet further.

The EC135 climbed out of the helipad zone, banked to the south and headed for the Hida mountain range.

22

SHINKANSEN BULLET TRAIN, EN-ROUTE NAGANO, JAPAN

The chief steward's cabin on that particular Shinkansen was situated right at the back of the bullet train. It was a snug little spot, not much larger than a cupboard really, and it was rare for the steward to be disturbed outside the departure and arrival times of the train at the various stations.

When the telephone rings in there it normally means trouble.

'There's a rat on the train,' the catering manager blurted out. 'It's just run through the restaurant car.'

The chief steward was astonished to hear this news. The trains were kept immaculately clean and he had never heard of such a thing in the ten years he had been working the Tokyo–Nagano route.

'I'll be right there,' he told his colleague. He put on his peaked hat, briefly checked his collar and tie in the mirror, and quit the cabin to head along the corridors towards the restaurant car.

When he got there he found a scene of regrettable confusion. A dozen or so passengers were clamouring to be heard as three or four of the catering staff tried to placate them.

'Now. Where is this creature?'

'In there.' The catering boss pointed to the kitchen.

A rat in the kitchen! The chief steward knew at that point that he had a really serious problem on his hands.

23

SHINKANSEN BULLET TRAIN, EN-ROUTE NAGANO, JAPAN

'Rabid Rat bites Bullet Train Dude' wasn't a terribly big file. It weighed in at a slender fifteen megabytes and was uploaded to YouTube in less than three minutes from the powerful processors on Cody's iPhone.

The 'upload complete' icon flashed on the screen and the boys knew it was now just a question of being processed onto the site. 'Doesn't look so busy today,' Sam chuckled, 'it'll be live in ten minutes.'

'Cool. I'll put it on Facebook and Vimeo as well,' Cody told him. 'And I'll tweet it. This one has to go global.'

In less than fifteen minutes the two American kids had placed the sixty second clip onto the most potent social networking sites on the planet. A tiny, bizarre incident on a fast-moving bullet train in Japan now had the potential to be seen by many millions of people.

'Let me see it one more time,' Sam demanded. Cody pressed play. The two boys cackled with laughter as they hunched over the clip. Over in the corner of the carriage, the huge ruddy-faced German guy had just returned from the toilet and rejoined his wife. The inspection clearly hadn't improved his mood; he was still clutching at his groin and muttering murderously about lawsuits and damages.

He glared at the two boys as he heard them sniggering. If only you knew, Cody thought, if only you knew.

24

Takumi and Riku scanned the tracks for guards or other observers, then they quickly pushed through the hole and ran for the cover of a stationary cargo train.

They dodged behind the huge steel wheels and looked up and down the station complex. On their previous attempt this had been as far as they got before they were spotted and ignominiously thrown out of the station.

'You think anyone saw us?' Takumi was by far the more nervous of the two. He hadn't even wanted to cut through the security fence but his mate Riku had been pretty persuasive.

'No. We're OK so far.' Riku was buzzing high on the sheer balls-out nerve of the enterprise. 'Let's shift.'

They moved cautiously through the cargo zone, hopping across the tracks and finding a good hiding place in an inspection pit cut into the ground.

Riku took out his mobile phone and shot some video of Takumi as he hunkered down in the bottom of the inspection pit. Takumi gave him a 'thumbs up' and a big smile even though deep down he was feeling stressed out and wired.

Riku turned the camera on himself:

'Made it through the fence,' he hissed in a stage whisper, 'so far OK!'

He turned off the video device.

Now all they had to do was wait. For the bullet train to arrive.

25

Casio felt a vibration against his thigh. The title track from 'Beast Wars' warbled thinly in the cab.

'What the . . . ?' Then he got it. It was the iPhone he had stolen from the American kid earlier that evening. Casio kept one hand on the steering wheel as he pulled the device from his pocket.

'Give me that.' Leonardo grabbed the iPhone. On the screen he saw the words 'Google Alert'.

There are six types of alert searches offered by Google and the 'News and Web' setting is the one that this iPhone was set for. As a wildlife fanatic, the eleven-year-old owner of the phone had come up with a bunch of gory keyword associations he was interested in hearing about:

'Bear Attack' was one of them.

That was the alert that was now showing on the phone. A police helicopter rescue station in Japan had released a terse communiqué to a local news station: 'Helicopter scrambled. Suspected bear attack in progress in the Hida mountain range.'

The news company had put it on their internet forum and it had flashed to servers all over the world.

'Some Google alert about a bear attack in Japan!' Leonardo said with a laugh. 'Nice phone, by the way, I think I'll keep it.'

Casio cursed, tried to snatch the iPhone back. The movement caused him to swerve across the alley.

A dark figure was stooping over a rubbish pile right in front of them.

'Look out!' Leonardo grabbed the wheel.

26

Roger Stansfield walked down the carriage back to his place. The commotion seemed to have died down a bit at the far end of the car and the big German guy was being comforted by his wife.

Saki—the girl who had lost her rat—was sitting there in her seat, fat tears dripping into the little empty cage.

The sight of her provoked a pang of guilt in the academic: he had been clumsy and stupid to spill that coffee. Forgetting about it in his hurry to call Yamada.

'I am so sorry,' he told the girl. Then he took out his handkerchief to dab at the bite wound on her thumb.

'I'm an animal lover myself,' he told her, 'the last thing I'd ever want to do would be to hurt a defenceless creature.'

'I have to catch him . . . can you help me catch him?' the girl begged.

'Leave it to the train managers,' Stansfield told her. 'They might find him if you're lucky.'

'They'll kill him!' Saki exclaimed.

Stansfield watched as the girl rushed off to chase her pet. She was still carrying the little cage but Stansfield couldn't imagine that it would easily be captured again.

There were myriad places to hide on a train such as this and rats were cunning creatures which would run to ground at the first sign of pursuit.

The girl would never see her pet again. He was sure of that.

27

Remo leapt for his life as the Hummer careered out of the shadows and slapped straight into the rubbish pile.

A tidal wave of fetid waste went airborne as he twisted his body into the jump. The evil looking snout of the 4x4 ploughed deep into the crap but Remo got away with a nasty knock on the hand.

Razor-sharp reflexes had saved the pig-boy. But the vehicle was a mess. The bonnet and windscreen were covered in slimy detritus; bits of festering fruit were packed into the front grille.

And the metal pole Remo used for turning over the rubbish had punched a hole through one of the front headlights. The glass was scattered amongst the trash.

Remo scrabbled to his feet as two characters emerged from the Hummer. The pig-boy felt his bowels quiver as he got a clearer look at the two men. Drug lord Leonardo and his scumbag son. This was the worst news. Ever. The pig-boy knew these two were capable of anything.

'You idiot!' Leonardo inspected the damage and cuffed his son savagely on the back of the neck.

'It was him,' Casio said, pointing at Remo. 'He broke the headlight.' The young thug picked up the metal pole and advanced menacingly on Remo.

Remo ducked as Casio swung the bar. Then he leapt off the rubbish pile and hightailed it down the alley as fast as he could run.

'Catch him!' Leonardo roared.

An instant later, Casio was in hot pursuit.

28

'Rabid Rat bites Bullet Train Dude' was taking off like wildfire. Two blog sites aimed at teenagers immediately featured it on their 'pick of the day' and an American TV network had already run it twice.

Kids were texting the link to their mates. Emails about it were zapping about the ether. The number of hits on YouTube was rising fast—from a thousand to a hundred thousand in minutes.

The word was spreading about the hilarious clip. And a ten-year-old American boy in Atlanta was about to watch it. His name was Donny Ordish and at that moment he was wolfing down a king-size hot dog while surfing the net on his smart phone.

Donny's Samsung was his most beloved possession. He'd saved his pocket money for two years to get it. Now he selected the text option as he heard an SMS coming in. It was from a schoolfriend and all it said was:

LOL . . . It had a link to YouTube attached to it.

Donny was chuckling even as the clip began: the sight of that huge German guy stabbing at the rat with his umbrella was something else. Then he snorted as he saw the rat dash up the German guy's leg.

'Dad. You gotta see this. This is so cool.'

He was still stuffing his face with that hot dog. Then it happened. Donny was laughing so much he inhaled a chunk of hot dog meat and it sealed off his windpipe like a plug in a drain.

Donny Ordish clutched at his throat and tried to breathe.

'Donny?' His father Frank jumped to his feet and slapped his son hard on the back.

Donny wasn't the only one whose world was about to be radically affected by the uploaded video.

The words 'Bullet Train' on Cody's uploaded video to Twitter had triggered a link on tweetalarm.com and fired off a message to trainspotter Nelson F. Muster.

Nelson followed up on the tweetalarm; watched the video with amusement.

Then his mind clicked on and he wondered if there was a station webcam which would show him the actual bullet train on which the incident had happened.

That would be cool.

But which bullet train had it happened on? There were dozens of the things speeding across the Japanese rail network at any moment.

He clicked back to the twitpic page, scrolling down from the video. The description box had nothing except for the video title. But then he found a hashtag that Cody had added: #NaganoBullet.

That was the clue he was looking for. They were on the Nagano bullet train.

His hand moved to the mouse and he googled Japanese Railway Timetables. Seconds later he had the English version of the website in front of him and it was a breeze to select the Tokyo–Nagano route.

He clicked through his list of webcams, swiftly finding the extensive array of Japanese station cameras on the route.

Nelson purred with excitement. It was shaping up into an interesting session.

30
THE ORDISH FAMILY HOME, ATLANTA, USA

It was all happening so fast. Every parent's worst nightmare.

Donny's father Frank watched in horror as his son continued to choke. A sensation of raw dread overwhelmed him as he realized his son wasn't kidding.

'Spit it out, Donny.' Frank struck Donny for a second time between the shoulder blades but the offending piece of hot dog was lodged down deep and it wasn't shifting from his windpipe.

Donny made a gurgling noise but no air was getting through. He stared at his father in mute horror, barely able to rationalize what was happening to him. His lips were already grey—his skin draining of colour and becoming rapidly as white as a corpse.

'Open your mouth!' Frank ordered him. He stared into the back of his son's throat, hoping to be able to see the lodged chunk of food and perhaps pick it out with his fingers.

But there was nothing to see.

Donny snatched at the tablecloth as he fell backwards. Plates and jugs cracked into smithereens as he hit the floor. Donny's mother heard the commotion, came running in from the kitchen.

'Call an ambulance!' Frank told her. She ran for the phone as Donny writhed on his back, his lips already turning blue, his eyes bulging out of their sockets as oxygen starvation began to shut his body down.

Frank was a customs officer. He had been trained by his department in first aid and had practised the Heimlich manoeuvre on a dummy. He picked up his son and positioned him in front of him, clasping his hands just beneath Donny's ribs.

31

Remo dashed up a narrow passageway, Leonardo's son closing on him with deadly intent.

The alley was one of the steepest in the slum, a walkway so precipitous that some sections even had a rope for pedestrians to pull themselves up.

Remo kept moving. Praying Casio would quickly tire.

The gradient was crazy, the steps slick with grungey mud and grime. He kept on running, climbing, his heart protesting with a needle ache as his ribcage shunted in and out.

A growing terror was overwhelming him. Leonardo's son was not tiring at all. He was so close Remo could hear his gold chains chinking as they flopped round his neck.

Remo turned a corner. Flatter ground. A wider street. He was hoping for some late night pedestrians, even a bunch of drunks might help him out if they recognized him.

But there was no one around. And Casio was still gaining.

Remo decided to head for the compound where he lived. The wall was high—he figured his pursuer might not be able to climb it.

Sprint. Push. Keep moving.

Turn uphill again. Keep pounding up that hillside, passing darkened shacks, the smell of woodsmoke, human sweat, and cheap liquor spewing out into the night.

Don't get caught. Outrun him or get the beating from hell.

32

SHINKANSEN BULLET TRAIN, EN-ROUTE NAGANO, JAPAN

The kitchen of the bullet train was a perfect rodent hiding zone.

A fact that the chief steward was now coming to terms with.

There were dozens of secret places there: in—or under—the ovens, fridges, and washing areas. The outraged diners had already voted with their feet, downing their coffees and teas and quitting the restaurant car to return to their seats.

'Did you see the size of that rat?' one of them was heard to exclaim. 'Big as a darn cat!'

'It's already bitten some poor man,' another muttered, 'he'll probably sue.'

'I can find him,' said a voice. Saki pushed her way through the other passengers. 'He's my pet.'

The chief steward gave her a chance. In fact he gave her several minutes of calling, whistling, and pleading with the elusive Brad to come back out to his cage. But the animal was well and truly freaked. He wasn't coming out for anyone—not even his kind-hearted owner. Not so much as a shiny pink nose was spotted.

'We have to fumigate,' the chief steward announced. 'I will go and inform the driver now. We'll radio ahead and get a fumigation team ready at the next station.'

'Please. Give me more time,' Saki pleaded, 'I'm sure he'll come out in a minute.'

'No more time,' the Chief Steward told her, 'I'm afraid we have to exterminate your pet.'

'Exterminate?' Saki put her hand to her mouth in horror.

33

THE ORDISH FAMILY HOME, ATLANTA, USA

Frank Ordish braced his arms around his son's chest. Then he tightened them abruptly as he had learned in the course. The movement was urgent and fast, but he didn't use maximum force—he knew he would break his son's ribs if he used all his strength.

Donny kind of spasmed. He was still making that awful keening noise, utterly unable to suck air into his lungs.

But nothing was expelled from his windpipe. That morsel of hot dog was firmly wedged.

'Hang on in there, Donny!' Frank urged his son. He could see the boy was losing consciousness, his eyes were getting fuzzy and unfocused.

Frank was getting close to panic. The situation was well out of control and he wasn't sure if he had done the Heimlich right. He couldn't quite remember the instructions he'd been given on the course.

Damn it! he raged at himself. Get your mind in gear! Wasn't there something about pressing upwards? Getting the hands underneath the ribcage somewhere?

His wife ran back into the room. She wailed as she saw Donny lying limply in her husband's arms.

'What did they say?' he asked her.

'Fifteen minutes.' *Fifteen minutes? Frank knew at that point that if he couldn't save his son then no one else was going to.*

He dragged Donny back to his feet. Flexed his arms back around the boy's chest again and interlocked his fingers in what he hoped was the right spot.

Just beneath the ribcage. Got to do it right this time. There might not be another chance.

34

Remo hurdled a drunk lying prone on the mud. A couple were making out in the shadows of a dark doorway.

He was still heading higher in the *favela*, running for his shack, but he didn't have much left in the tank. His legs felt blown out and he could almost feel Casio's hot breath on his neck.

Darting into ever more obscure alleyways, using his intimate knowledge of the slum, hoping to lose Casio in the maze.

Then he saw the high wall of the compound. Safety might be at hand if he could only get up it.

His legs were cramping up. His body had given all it had to give.

A final desperate move. He stepped up on an empty oil barrel, leapt for a handhold, got his fingers curled around the wall. A quick pull up and his knee was hooked onto the lip. Then he was rolling up and over, falling down the far side and landing in a pile of rotting waste.

The compound was an urban pig-pen and this was where one of Remo's clients had let him build a shack. The sleeping creatures scattered with grunts of alarm as he landed amongst them.

He turned. Looked up, his heart sinking as he saw Casio make it onto the top of the wall. But then, the thug lost his balance . . .

Casio crashed hard onto compacted soil from a height of three metres, both arms outstretched. The wind was driven from his body.

His left arm broke with a dry, reedy snap.

35

Nelson watched with pleasure as the Kariuzawa Station webcam fuzzed into life. The image was not full screen but the resolution was pretty good.

It was a satisfactory viewpoint, a high shot revealing all the platforms.

The scene was quiet at that moment. No trains to be seen, just a few passengers milling about the platforms. All he had to do was wait until the bullet train pulled in.

Then he saw something strange:

Two boys sneaked across the bottom of the shot and hid behind a stack of concrete girders which had been stacked next to one of the platforms.

Nelson's curiosity was instantly aroused.

Who were those kids? And what were they up to?

They were obviously making an effort not to be seen.

Nelson decided he would call his friend and fellow train-spotter Paco to tell him about it.

He clicked on Skype and began the call. He had completely forgotten about the coffee sitting on the gas.

The water had just boiled up into the top section and the empty bottom section of the coffee maker was now getting the full force of the gas ring.

Little by little, the metal was beginning to glow red hot.

36

Frank Ordish used all his force this time. He grunted as he performed the manoeuvre, driving his interlocked hands up and back, squashing Donny's lungs in a violent movement and trying not to think about what it could do to the boy's ribcage.

This time was different. There was a kind of rushing squeak of air expelled from Donny's mouth—

And a solid chunk of hot dog flew across the room.

The two of them fell back in a heap on the floor. Donny was drinking in air by the lungful as Frank let out a huge sigh of pure relief. Donny's mother joined them in a group hug and they held each other tight as Donny gradually regained his composure.

When they had recovered a bit, Frank pulled his son to his feet.

'What the hell were you looking at?' Frank asked his son, picking up his smart phone. 'What was so damn funny it nearly killed you?'

Donny was shamefaced: 'A video of some rat biting a guy on a train.'

Frank snorted. That was the final word. He had nearly lost his son because of some kooky viral video about a rat. Donny's mother went to brew up some tea and the three of them sat at the kitchen table as Frank logged on to Twitter and began to compose a tweet.

'Biggest scare ever,' he wrote. 'Life is so fragile.'

He pressed the 'tweet' button and sent his message out to the six hundred and thirty-odd followers he had around the world.

The passengers had been informed that there would be a small delay at Kariuzawa. They were not informed that the cause was a rat running loose on the train.

The chief steward supervised the operation as the defumigating machine was lifted on board the train, wheeled into position and connected to a mains supply coming from the station offices.

Three operators wearing gas masks and white protection suits sealed all the doors to the catering car, quickly taped plastic sheeting up to isolate the kitchen zone and got straight to work.

A small quantity of sulfuryl fluoride gas was injected. The rat would be dead within minutes, the fumigators assured the chief steward.

The kitchen area would have to remain sealed for twenty-four hours. No further food would be served but the passengers would just have to lump it.

The chief steward had been sweating with tension as the rodent had been eliminated but he felt he had made the right decision. A fifteen minute delay was a big deal by bullet train standards but he could justify it to his bosses back in Tokyo.

A live rat on board? Well it just wasn't on!

In any case that rat was now lying well and truly dead somewhere in the gas-filled zone which was the kitchen area.

The girl—Saki—who had wept so copiously as she watched the extermination team come on board, had retreated back to her seat where she sat in a sort of stunned and miserable silence with her empty cage.

The chief steward checked his watch. Time was rolling by. They would have to be leaving soon. Very soon.

38

Remo watched as Casio lay gulping for air in that filthy pig yard. He was curled up on the ground, his face ghostly white in the moonlight.

'This is all your fault . . . ' the thug gasped. Remo was itching to do a runner. He feared that Leonardo would quickly be on the scene.

But he knew he couldn't leave Casio lying like that. If they saw him defenceless, the pigs might attack and attempt to eat him. Remo knew only too well how vicious they could be. They would eat literally anything organic.

And that included human flesh.

So he shooed the inqusitive pigs away and waited the couple of minutes it took Casio to recover his breath. He watched as the thug explored the damage to his arm, letting out an agonized cry of pain as he attempted to flex it.

It was well and truly banged up. Even in the moonlight Remo could see that the bone was grotesquely fractured. The top part of his arm was twisted into a right angle where it should have been straight.

'What street is this?' Casio gasped. 'I got to get my dad here—get me to hospital.' Remo told him the location and watched as the thug used his good arm to pull out his mobile.

After the call he helped Casio out onto the street, determined to make off as soon as he could.

But as they left the compound the drug lord's Hummer was already pulling up.

Remo's heart sank. It was too late to run.

39

The search and rescue helicopter flew east from the Nagano base, gaining altitude as it went. It was an exceptionally clear day, and as they reached a height of one thousand five hundred metres above sea level they could see for almost one hundred kilometres across the serrated summits of the Hida mountain range.

The peaks were snowbound, the lakes below glittering with the deep azure of meltwater. The temperature registered on the external sensor was twenty-six degrees below freezing. The co-pilot put the cockpit heater on full and trimmed the rotors for maximum fuel efficiency as they cruised rapidly to the area where the bullet train tracks snaked around the end of the range.

As soon as they reached the target zone the rescue heli began a classic search and rescue grid pattern, flying five kilometre quadrants then repositioning to search a new corridor.

The crew were all experienced in the fine art of spotting injured people from the air but they knew they were fighting the odds on this mission. The mountainous terrain was just too thickly forested to spot the tiny figure of a human being. If they found the injured academic it would be by luck rather than flying skill.

'We need some smoke to find this guy,' the pilot commented.

'Too right.'

But there was not the slightest trickle of smoke to be seen.

Takumi and Riku raised their heads cautiously from their hiding place and watched the bullet train intently.

They were positioned on the blind side of the train, the side opposite to the platform, but they could see immediately that there was a lot of activity going on.

'That's not normal,' Riku said, 'something's not right about this.'

Through the undercarriage they could see some sort of operation in progress in the centre of the train. A small team in white overalls had dragged a machine festooned with pipes and cables across towards the bullet train.

The duo knew from previous observations that the train would normally spend about three and a half minutes at the platform. They also knew that the station was covered by numerous security cameras so the odds were stacked against them.

'What are they doing?' Riku whispered.

'No idea. But it's going to give us a good distraction. Let's move.'

'There's too many people on the platform. We should wait.'

The two boys waited—their hearts in their mouths. They had spent many hours studying the trains that came through Kariuzawa, had already figured the weak spot—the gap between the carriages.

Riku was so wired he felt himself in a state of hyper awareness. His heart thundered against his ribs. They were so close now. If only they could make it up onto the roof.

41

Back at the pig yard Leonardo was checking out his son's broken arm, tutting with anger as he saw the severity of the break. The boy had lost all his bluster. He was shivering with pain and shock.

Leonardo turned to Remo.

The street kid nearly wet himself when he saw the look of pure venom in the gangster's eyes.

'I have always believed,' Leonardo told Remo softly, 'in an eye for an eye, a tooth for a tooth.'

So saying, he grabbed Remo by the elbow and the three of them stumbled over to the Hummer.

Remo was chucked into the back seat and the Hummer took off like a bat out of hell. It bucked and bounced across the pot-holed tracks of the slum, Casio whimpering like a whipped dog as his broken arm was jolted about.

Remo was cursing himself. Why had he been so soft? Why hadn't he taken the opportunity to flee when Casio was lying injured?

But that wasn't how he was. Remo would never walk away from someone who needed help—even if they were a deadly enemy.

Minutes later they skidded to a stop in a heavily guarded yard which Remo figured had to be one of Leonardo's drug fortresses.

'You're staying here,' Leonardo said, leading him to a foul-smelling cell. 'I'm getting my boy patched up then we're coming back to sort you out.'

He threw Remo into the cell and padlocked the metal door behind him.

42

HIDA MOUNTAIN RANGE, JAPAN

Professor Yamada heard the thwock—thwock—thwock of the approaching rescue helicopter when it was still two kilometres from the ridge.

He thought about his options. How could he attract attention?

The only tool he had that was of the slightest use was a cigarette lighter and he could scarcely light a fire in the very tree he was using for sanctuary.

Instead he pulled his sweatshirt over his head. Unfortunately it was dark green, which he knew would make it harder to spot.

Then the rotor noise increased dramatically. The heli was flying almost directly overhead. It was so close that the professor could see the individual rivets on the under-carriage of the aircraft.

'H . . . h . . . h-hey!' Yamada waved his arms frantically in the air, the sweatshirt getting caught in the branches almost immediately.

In any case the heli didn't even slow down as it flew over his location, and from the fast receding sound of the rotors it was evident the pilots had chosen another area to search.

Yamada's heart plummeted as he heard the rotor wash fade away to a distant rumble across the huge valley.

43

Takumi and Riku reached the side of the train.

Takumi went first, swarming up the gap in a lithe movement and using the steel-clad cables which connected each carriage as a handhold.

He looked back. Riku was struggling to make it onto the roof. He wasn't as tall as Takumi and he couldn't reach up high enough to grasp the cables and pull himself up.

Takumi held down his hand and took a firm hold on his buddy. He pulled him up smoothly onto the roof. The duo immediately hunkered down next to a pantograph—one of the spring-loaded devices which transferred electricity to the train from the overhead cable.

They were keeping themselves as flat to the roof as they could to avoid detection. Takumi took out his mobile and he filmed a quick fifteen seconds of video of his friend lying on the roof.

The two friends stared at each other in delight to have got so far.

Now it was just a question of luck.

Would they be spotted or not?

They knew the chief steward would normally have to check the roof out before the train pulled away.

Takumi checked his watch. The minutes were ticking past. What was going on with this train? Maybe they had already been spotted on a security camera.

The boys lay still and hoped for the best.

44

Remo had heard the rumours about Leonardo's cells.

About the people who were locked up there and never seen again.

The desire to scream for help was overwhelming but he knew he would pay a terrible price if he did it. Casio seemed determined to exact revenge for that broken arm. And the more he provoked them the worse it would be.

He just had to pray that he would somehow emerge from this situation alive.

He had a quick check around the cell but there was absolutely no question of forcing an escape. The metal door was robust enough to resist a charging rhino and the walls were as solid as rock.

A double set of bars sealed the window.

Then he heard something from the cell next door. *The sound of someone crying. A girl, it seemed.*

He craned his neck, saw that there was a small air vent connecting the two cells. It was way above his head height but by jumping up he could grip onto the little alcove that supported the plastic grille.

He did it, pulling himself up with a strenuous move of his arms. He stared through the grille and found his hunch was right; it *was* a girl, eight or nine years old at a guess, curled up on a foam mat on the clay floor of her cell and weeping desolate tears of profound fear.

The sight of this poor girl twisted his heart. Who were these monsters? Was there no limit to the misery they were prepared to inflict?

'Hey!' he whispered. 'What's your name?'

45

At that moment, in one of Rio's western suburbs, a cop was driving back from an abortive late night operation. Her name was Juliana Amadeu, a sergeant based with the city's heavily overworked drug enforcement unit.

She had been with a bunch of her colleagues since midnight, staking out a warehouse which was rumoured to be a cocaine depot. But the tip off had been a false alarm and they'd abandoned the job after a few hours.

It was halfway through the night now but the ambitious young officer wasn't thinking of quitting yet. She actually enjoyed working night shifts—knowing that that was when the action really kicked off.

She was almost back to her office when she felt her mobile vibrate. A Twitter message. Juliana was addicted to Twitter, followed almost a thousand people from all over the world, and she couldn't resist taking a look:

'Biggest scare ever. Life is so fragile.'

Juliana thought about the tweet—and Frank Ordish, its creator. It sounded serious. A world away from the facile, trivial bleatings of most of the twitterers she followed.

That was the first thing. The second was that she actually *cared* about Customs Inspector Ordish. Just thinking about him brought a warm grin to Juliana's face; his sense of humour had enlivened an otherwise dull US

Customs Service delegation to Rio and if he hadn't been married back home well . . . that might have been another story.

She pulled over and stopped the car, tweeting back: 'Greetings from Rio. Hope you OK?'

46

Nelson clicked on Skype, putting on his headset and mic as he did so. Seconds later he was connected to his trainspotting buddy Paco who was online in his den in a garden shed in Austin, Texas.

'Dude, check out the Kariuzawa station webcam on the bullet train site. You have *got* to take a look at what's happening there.'

'Errr. OK. Give me a moment.'

The sound quality on Skype had improved dramatically in recent months. Nelson could even hear his buddy mouse-clicking on the links which would take him swiftly to the site.

Then came the voice:

'OK. Errr . . . I see a bullet train stuck in the station. So what?'

'Look closer, Paco. Right in the middle. On the top.'

'Still not getting it.'

'There's two local kids hunched up on the roof behind one of the pantographs. They're gonna surf the bullet.'

'No way! Yeah, I got them. You think this is real? I mean I thought those bullet train surfers were, like, urban legends or something.'

'They're real, dude. And I saw 'em first. I'm gonna grab a few freeze frames of this and put them on my blog.'

47

PARADA DE LUCAS, RIO DE JANEIRO, BRAZIL

The girl looked up at Remo, shocked to see that she was being watched through the grille. He saw deep suspicion in her eyes and he wasn't surprised: being snatched away from your family and chucked into a foul smelling prison cell at the age of eight or nine isn't likely to increase your ability to trust strangers.

'I'm a prisoner too,' he whispered. 'They've locked me up in here just like you.'

The girl sniffed away her tears and wiped her sleeve across her grubby cheeks. Then she stood up, peering up at the ventilation hole and trying to get a fix on who this new person was.

'My name's Remo,' he told her, 'what's yours?'

'Ester.'

'Why have they put you in there?'

'I don't know . . .'

The abduction had been shockingly fast; the slightly built little girl never stood a chance. Two masked men leapt from a truck as she went with a bucket to collect water from a tap near her shanty home. Before onlookers had a chance to react they had bundled the terrified girl into the back seat and spirited her away. One of the men pushed her head down as the pick-up drove away. His hand smelt of cigarettes and engine oil.

'Don't try and scream,' they told her as they threw her in the cell. 'If you do we'll have to cut off your tongue.'

'Can you help me?' she pleaded with Remo. 'I want to go home . . .'

48

SHINKANSEN BULLET TRAIN, EN-ROUTE NAGANO, JAPAN

'Are we ready to go?' The station manager was as keen as anyone to get the train on the move. Other Shinkansen schedules would be affected by their delay at Kariuzawa and he was eager not to be reprimanded by the control centre at Tokyo.

The chief steward took a hasty look up and down the platform then answered yes. He bade farewell to the station manager and jumped on board.

In that moment he made a big mistake. The stress of the rat incident had scrambled his mind just enough to cause him to forget his routine security check of the train.

He should have checked the television monitor mounted on the wall.

He should have made a visual confirmation that no one had climbed onto the roof.

But he didn't. There was just too much pressure and he had simply forgotten his mental checklist of things to do.

The chief steward went to his cabin and radioed through to the driver.

'All set,' he told the senior engineer.

Moments later he felt the train jerk as the motors locked in.

The Nagano bullet train recommenced its journey.

49

Remo had been holding on to the little ledge for several minutes, chatting to the young girl. Now he couldn't hold on any longer.

'I'll talk to you again later,' he told his new friend. 'Just stay positive and everything will work out OK.'

He dropped back to the floor of his cell, rubbing his arms vigorously to get the circulation going.

The reassuring words had come easily. But in reality he knew her situation was truly desperate.

It wasn't hard for Remo to work out what was going on. Kidnappings were frighteningly common in Rio, sometimes to extort money from wealthy families, other times to force family members to act as drug couriers.

Now he thought about her situation, feeling his anger harden to a steel core. He had seen many injustices in his life, everyone who lived on the marginal edges of Brazilian society witnessed them on a daily basis. But this girl was so utterly innocent, and her fears would be so raw.

To be ripped away from her mother, her father, at such an age was a truly despicable crime.

He leapt back up to the grille, hissed to get her attention once again. 'If they don't kill me, I'll do what I can to help you,' he told her.

He took off the golden cross he wore around his neck and passed it to her through the vent.

'Thank you.' His words—and his gift—provoked a flood of grateful tears from Ester. *If they don't kill me?* The stark nature of his own words haunted Remo as he waited to learn his fate.

50

Nelson was watching his computer screen with a growing sense of excitement as he saw the train start to move. The Japanese kids were still hunkered down on the roof, but he was sure as he could be that they were going to try and surf the bullet once it started moving.

'OK! The train's pulling out of the station,' he told Paco who was still on the Skype connection.

'Yeah. I can see it. Those guys are in for the ride of their lives. Hey, maybe we can catch them on a webcam at the next stop? What's the next station?'

'Yeah, that'd be neat! Let me see . . . ' Nelson swiftly checked the bullet train website for the timetable. 'Actually that's the last stop before Nagano. But we might still see them go through the next station . . . '

'Excellent!'

Nelson could feel the adrenaline flowing. Bullet train surfers! How cool was this?

He had completely forgotten about the little collection of pills. And he had completely forgotten about the coffee.

51

ON BOARD SHINKANSEN BULLET TRAIN, EN-ROUTE NAGANO, JAPAN

The rat had been hiding behind a dishwasher when the first whiff of gas had begun to filter from the fumigation unit. With a sense of smell many hundreds of times more acute than a human, the small rodent was at first almost overcome by the effects of the Sulfuryl Fluoride.

But this creature was tough. And resourceful. Even with its eyes streaming with fluid it could still see enough to flee.

As the fumigation team sprayed the noxious cocktail, the rat was on the move, scurrying along the back wall of the kitchen, moving just ahead of the deadly cloud. It pushed into a dark hole leading to the cavity beneath the floor.

The fumigators may have imagined that their grisly work would be inescapable, but they weren't reckoning on the extraordinary instincts for survival that has enabled *Rattus norvegicus* to become one of the most widespread species on the planet.

The rat found a cable duct and scampered off into the floor cavity beneath the driver's compartment.

There it waited for the effects of the gas to pass.

52

Remo heard the rumble of a powerful engine pulling back into the yard. Through the bars of his cell he saw it was Leonardo's Hummer and his heart clenched at the sight of it.

Whatever was coming, he prayed it was going to be fast.

He pulled back into the shadows as Leonardo climbed out of the front to be greeted by two of his guards. There was no sign of Casio—Remo guessed Leonardo had left him at casualty to get his arm sorted out.

Would they break Remo's arm in revenge? Or maybe both of them. Wasn't that what Leonardo had meant when he said 'an eye for an eye . . . '?

Remo had known much pain in his life but he would never be able to work with a broken arm. He and his mother would starve if he couldn't collect the pigswill.

He heard one of the guards say, 'I'll bring him out.'

So. This was it. Remo decided he would say a couple of final words of encouragement to Ester in the cell next door. He jumped up, holding on to the little ledge and whispered to wake her:

'Hey . . . Ester!'

Then he heard a noise at the barred window of his cell.

Leonardo was staring in. And his face was pure rage.

'So!' he hissed. 'You want to poke your nose into my business do you, boy?' Moments later Remo heard the sound of the padlock being released and a guard dragged him roughly out of the cell.

53

Nelson was just about to click on the webcam for the next station on the bullet train route when he paused.

He could smell burning.

Then a few neurons pulsed in his brain. Ping! A twist in his gut as he realized what he had forgotten.

The coffee!

Nelson rushed out of his room and headed for the kitchen where he saw that the coffee maker was now glowing red hot on the range.

The logical thing to have done would have been to simply turn off the gas and wait an hour or so for the metal coffee maker to cool off.

But Nelson was desperate to get back to those images of the bullet train. In the heat of the moment he grabbed hold of the handle of the coffee maker. Only then did he realize that the bakelite handle was itself red hot.

Nelson dropped the coffee maker. His fingers were badly burned. It bounced off the edge of the cooker and spilt the entire liquid contents of the pot down his thighs.

'Shoot!'

Nelson F. Muster let out a howl of pain.

Remo didn't resist, just let himself be jostled out into the yard where Leonardo waited for him with a face like thunder.

'You've been having a nice chat with our little guest have you? What did she tell you?' Leonardo demanded.

'Nothing, sir.'

He slapped Remo hard on the cheek—a blow savage enough to bring stars to his eyes.

'You must be crazy to talk to her, boy. You don't know what you're getting into. Did she tell you her name? Her address? What else do you *know*?'

A further blow followed to the back of the head. Remo fell to his knees, dizzy with the impact.

'She didn't tell me anything, I swear.'

'Did she give you a message for the police? For her parents?'

Remo shook his head, crying bitterly. Leonardo went to a corner of the yard and conducted an urgent conversation with one of his henchmen.

When he came back Remo was expecting a further explosion of violence; he braced himself for another blow— but none came. Instead the drug lord walked up close to him and told him gently, 'We're going for a drive.'

Remo felt his hands pulled behind his back. A cord was tied around his wrists. A hood was placed over his head and he was slung into the Hummer.

Now Remo knew. This wasn't some punishment beating. The stakes had just got a lot higher. This was going to be something much more serious.

55

The acceleration was incredible, the bullet train was running at about eighty kilometres an hour—fast enough that it was even now a struggle to stand upright on the roof.

But the boys were determined to give it a try.

Riku took out his mobile and clicked through the options until he got the camera activated. The sunlight was too bright to see much on the little screen but he pointed it at Takumi as his friend managed to get to his feet in a classic surfing stance.

The high voltage electric cables delivering power to the pantographs were zooming past now at more than a hundred kilometres an hour just centimetres above his head.

'Yeeeeeees!' Takumi yelled. He flashed a thumbs up at his friend then quickly crouched back down again to take the camera and return the favour.

Then Riku stood up, finding it harder to stay upright now as the train's speed had increased notably.

One hundred and forty kilometres an hour. Riku felt he was about to be blown right off his feet.

Then he saw Takumi was trying to yell something at him.

'What?'

'Tunnel!' Takumi shouted.

The boys ducked down, laughing hysterically as the train ripped into the tunnel.

56

Eight-year-old Ester watched miserably from the bars of her cell as Remo was driven off into the night.

The sense of isolation was unbearable.

Her one friend and ally was gone. She was alone again with these violent and unpredictable men. No one to whisper words of encouragement. No one to tell her that everything would work out OK, that she would feel the warmth of her mother's arms once more.

Just the clawing fear inside her. The terror of helplessness. And the sense that the clock was ticking down to . . .

To what?

That was the worst thing. This eight-year-old girl had no idea what these men were planning to do with her.

The sound of Leonardo's Hummer faded into the night. All she could hear was the muttered conversation of the two guards out in the yard, the click of a cigarette lighter followed by the acrid smell of rough tobacco.

She remembered the little pendant that Remo had slipped through the ventilation vent, took it out of her pocket and looked at it closely. The gold was worn, the edges of the cross smoothed down by age and devotion. She began to pray, holding the little cross in her hand and thinking of her sister Mariana.

Leonardo had told her her sister was doing a job for him. But what type of job? What could they want with Mariana?

Ester prayed for her sister. And wondered where on earth she was.

57

Roger Stansfield was watching the countryside speed past, feeling more guilty than ever and fervently wishing he had taken an aeroplane to Nagano.

His accidental scalding of the rat had provoked an extraordinary chain of events—ending with a massive delay for the train and the fumigation of the dining car.

He checked his mobile but there was no news from the professor. Had he been rescued? Was he still being stalked by that bear? Stansfield texted him to find out.

Moments later he got the reply:

No rescue. Still in tree. Bear won't leave!

The plaintive text provoked a huge wave of sympathy for his colleague. How much longer would Yamada have to wait? The stress must be terrible.

More than anything, Stansfield wanted to help. If the rescue wasn't happening then maybe there was another way to be of assistance? Something he could think of to scare off the bear?

Roger Stansfield gazed distractedly at the passing scenery; a whole bunch of half-baked ideas floating around in his mind. Something about the fumigation was trying to spark a thought deep inside his brain. Something about chemicals and the fact that Yamada was an insect collector . . .

Then he got it.

'Yes!' Stansfield gasped out loud as his mind finally made the connections.

He had an idea that might save Yamada's life.

58

Nelson F. Muster chewed on his tongue as he daubed cold water on his thighs. The flesh was getting more tender with every passing minute, the blisters filling with fluid as the scalded skin reacted to the shock of the boiling coffee.

He had never known pain like it.

Nelson picked up a flannel and mopped the sweat from his face. His hands were shuddering. The accident had triggered an anxiety attack.

What should he do? Get some ice? Call his mom? Call an ambulance? A cab? Ignore it? The options whirled through his mind as he gobbled down a couple of Tylenol to take the edge off the pain.

Apart from anything else he was desperate to get back to his computer to see what was happening to those two kids on the bullet train.

Ping. Ping. He heard the distinctive warble of the Skype Fone. He pulled his shorts back up and limped back to his room to grab the headset.

On the screen all he could see was the empty station of Kariuzawa. The kids were already on their way to becoming legends and all Nelson could think about was the pain in his legs.

Of all the days for an accident to happen.

Had to be today.

Just when the action was kicking off.

Nelson wished he could wind back the clock.
Too late now.

59

The answer to Ester's question regarding the whereabouts of her sister Mariana was as follows: she was sitting in seat 45a on a Boeing 737 which would shortly be landing in Seattle.

In her belly were one and a half kilos of cocaine.

This was Leonardo's plan; this was why Ester had been kidnapped—so that eighteen-year-old Mariana could be forced into acting as an illegal drug courier—a 'mule' smuggling cocaine into the USA.

She had no choice. She had to go through with the job. Even though she hated drugs and all the misery they caused and had never so much as touched a cigarette or a drop of alcohol in her life.

Mariana had no doubt they would follow through on their threats to kill Ester if she tried to denounce them to the police, or back out of the mission.

Her parents had been paralysed with terror. A kidnapping like this one was every slum parent's worst fear. They were poor people, with no high up contacts to call on. *They didn't even dare tell the police.*

Leonardo had made Mariana swallow more than two hundred plastic capsules of the drug—each one containing a tiny quantity of the precious powder. Swallowing them had been hell. Mariana's throat was red raw. Then they had given her a special drug so that the capsules would stay in her stomach. Once she reached the USA, a second drug would kick start her digestive system again so the drugs could be retrieved.

Mariana felt the jet engines tremble as they throttled back. A wave of fear engulfed her. The aircraft was beginning its descent. The real test would soon begin.

60

'Hey. It's me.' Paco's voice came through loud and clear. 'I got the link for that station webcam site if you want to check it out.'

'Listen, Paco. I got a problem here, dude. I spilled a whole load of boiling coffee down my legs. You think I have to go see a doctor?'

'What? You gotta get that treated, man. You could get some kind of infection . . . gangrene or something.'

'*Gangrene?*' Nelson had a sudden flash vision of his legs turning black, of the wounds oozing with an evil flow of green pus.

'But what about those guys on the train?' he continued. 'I don't want to miss the action.'

'I'll record it all,' Paco reassured him. 'You won't miss a thing.'

Nelson felt salty drips of sweat run into his eyes. He lifted his T-shirt and dabbed at them as he muttered a stream of obscenities.

'All right. I'll get in a cab and go to the hospital.'

Nelson took a last longing look at his computer screens then rushed down the stairs to the street.

There was a cab rank close by where he could get a ride to the hospital.

61

Remo tried not to pass out with the fear, tried to keep a grip on himself as the Hummer rattled on its way. Leonardo and his guard said little in the front, just a few murmured words from time to time and nothing that made any sense to their captive.

Where were they taking him? The tension was unbearable.

The pig-boy was stunned at the speed that things had gone sour for him. Misfortune is like lightning, he thought; it strikes where it will and no man is immune to it. Just a short time earlier he had been going about his business, collecting his last sack of swill of the day and planning on going home to his little shack.

Now he was tied up in the back of a drug baron's vehicle in fear of his life. He couldn't even get a message to his mother on the other side of town.

She was all too aware of the risks her son's work involved. Violence was an ever present possibility in the tinder box environment of Rio's slums.

In the distance Remo could hear a distinctive sound . . . like a huge great grinding machine.

At the same time a putrid smell began to filter into the vehicle.

Both seemed familiar to Remo but he was so disorientated and freaked out by his situation that he couldn't—for the moment—figure it out.

What WAS that sound?

62

SHINKANSEN BULLET TRAIN, EN-ROUTE NAGANO, JAPAN

Riku and Takumi both ducked down as the train rushed into the tunnel, the temperature falling incredibly fast as the cool, damp air hit them. It was like putting your hand into a freezer, Riku thought, really breathtakingly cold and rather thrilling.

'Yeeeeeee—harrrgh!'

Takumi screamed with adrenaline and excitement as the walls of the tunnel rushed past at breakneck speed.

Both boys knew there was no way the passengers would hear them above the engine noise as it reverberated from the tunnel walls in a thunderous roar.

In the adrenaline pumping exhilaration of the first minutes, the boys had not paid much attention to the rapidly dropping temperature that they were now experiencing.

In fact it was the one factor that they had not taken into account at all.

Both were wearing nothing more than a T-shirt and denim jeans.

As the train hit one hundred and fifty kilometres an hour Riku felt his fingers beginning to go numb.

'Can't feel my fingers!' he yelled to Takumi.

Takumi merely nodded back. His face was locked in a grimace of pain as the cold continued to bite.

Then Riku felt his eyes freezing together as the train accelerated yet more.

63

Mariana the reluctant drug courier was so wired up with nerves that she jumped out of her skin when the captain's voice came up on the aircraft speaker system.

'Ladies and gentlemen. This is the captain here on the flight deck. As you've probably realized, we are well into our descent into Seattle International Airport . . . '

Mariana stared out of the window at the steely grey Pacific ocean as the aircraft banked round across the sea to begin its final approach. In the distance she could see the city of Seattle.

Her mind was buzzing with the instructions she had been given by Leonardo and the drug cartel. She couldn't afford to forget a single thing.

They had given her the plane ticket. Some cash to survive on in Seattle for a few days. Briefed her endlessly on what to say, how to act, if she was questioned. They promised nothing would go wrong but Mariana had heard the stories, horrific tales of girls who had had a package burst inside them, leading to a certain and terrible death through overdose.

Then there was the question of getting through customs and immigration in the USA.

It's not easy to keep cool when you have one and a half kilos of cocaine in your stomach.

Mariana fingered her rosary beads and whispered a prayer for the thousandth time that day.

64

Juliana Amadeu got a follow-up text from Frank Ordish in the US explaining what had happened to his son with the choking incident.

Just as she was composing the words to text him back, the policewoman saw something that made her heart trip:

Leonardo Feola's blinged-up Hummer raced past her and took a right turn at some lights.

Leonardo was a big dealer on the Rio drug scene but he was wary as a fox. Juliana and her colleagues had been hunting him for years but he always dealt through intermediaries, middlemen who would take the heat when the agency got close.

To bust him they would have to catch him red-handed, with enough incriminating evidence to put him away for good.

So where was he going in the middle of the night? This was a great lead for Juliana. He would certainly be up to something dodgy.

Juliana started up the engine and pulled out fast. She took the same turn as the Hummer and breathed a sigh of relief as she saw Leonardo's car in the distance.

As she drove it occurred to her . . .

If she hadn't stopped to reply to that Twitter message she never would have seen the Hummer.

Juliana kept her eye on Leonardo's car and radioed back to base to ask for some back-up.

65

NELSON MUSTER'S NEIGHBOURHOOD, SEATTLE, USA

Nelson hurried down the street to the cab rank where he saw to his relief that two taxis were waiting. He was sweating with the exertion of moving so fast, blinking at the unaccustomed daylight.

'I need a ride to the hospital,' Nelson told the first driver. 'I got cash.'

The cab driver gave him a seasoned look. He was used to dealing with drunkards and weirdos and this stressed-out looking kid was obviously some sort of oddball with his brown-stained shorts and his flip-flops.

'I'm booked,' the cab driver told him.

He didn't like the look of this freaky kid. There was this crazy expression on his face which was frankly scary. And those odd stains on his shorts? It looked as if Nelson had soiled himself.

'But I burned myself,' Nelson told him, lowering the shorts so he could see the livid flesh. 'Whole pot of coffee went over my legs.'

'I don't wanna know your problems,' the driver told him.

His window closed with an electronic whine.

'Hey! I'm in pain here!' Nelson yelled, banging hard on the roof of the cab. 'I gotta get to hospital before I get gangrene, man.'

Nelson moved to the second cab, fixed the driver with a desperate stare. 'How about you? You gonna take me to the emergency? I gotta genuine problem here.'

The second cab driver didn't even respond. He just took one look at Nelson, pulled away from the rank and melted into the traffic flow.

66

HIDA MOUNTAIN RANGE, JAPAN

The professor had slipped into black despair; the helicopter had made no return sweep to his location and he remained at bay, stuck up a tree and feeling ridiculous in the middle of nowhere.

The bear was still hanging around, claws ripping at the bark in a disturbing fashion and staring at him from time to time. What did it want? When would it leave?

Yamada felt his mobile vibrate. Another text coming through. It was from Roger Stansfield and it consisted of just one word:

FORMALDEHYDE?

Yamada got the context instantly and he wondered how on earth he hadn't already thought of it. He had a two hundred and fifty millilitre bottle of formaldehyde in his rucksack, a potent poison which he used routinely in his 'killing jar' for despatching insects.

It was a basic part of any insect hunter's kit.

And a powerful weapon if used in the right way.

If the bear attacked again, the professor realized, he could throw the contents of the bottle into the creature's face. It would be agony when it hit the eyes, buying him some precious time.

There was only one small problem: Yamada had thrown off the rucksack during the first chase and it was now in the undergrowth on the other side of the glade.

Then he heard a chilling sound. The bear had decided to climb the tree.

67

Back in Rio, Juliana Amadeu was still tailing Leonardo's Hummer and now she saw the drug lord take a right into one of Rio's illegal waste tips.

A place notorious for accepting toxic waste.

She drove up a nearby hillside road and nosed her car into some shadows. She could look down into the dump from the position; it was a good spot to keep an eye on the situation.

What on earth was Leonardo doing?

Juliana had a small pair of surveillance binoculars in the glovebox and she pulled them out to get a better look. Down at the dump she could now see Leonardo and a meaty looking character next to him who she figured must be one of his henchmen.

They were talking to the site operators. Then a whole bunch of money changed hands.

Really quite a wad.

What was this? A drug exchange? Or was it something else? Then the cop got a sick feeling in her stomach.

A tied-up figure had been brought from the car. It looked too small to be an adult.

It's a kid, she realized. With a hood on his head. But what are they going to *do* to him?

The aircraft shuddered as the wheels touched down. Mariana braced herself as the engines roared into reverse thrust.

The young Brazilian girl had always dreamed of travelling and seeing the world. But doing it as a drug courier was never part of that plan.

The seat-belt sign pinged off. Mariana pulled her hand baggage from an overhead locker and queued to quit the plane. She tried hard not to attract attention, didn't meet anyone's eye, bit back the tears of misery that threatened to come at any moment.

There was an excited buzz amongst the passengers that surrounded her. How she envied them, preparing to meet loved ones at the gate, returning home, starting a new adventure. Free of worries. Free of fear.

All she had to look forward to was the ordeal of passing through customs. If they caught her then her life was effectively over.

How many years prison would she get. Fifteen? Twenty? A spasm of icy terror clutched at her guts as she contemplated it.

She walked slowly through the airport corridors. It all felt so weird, so unreal. And if it was bad for her, then how would it be for her little sister . . .

Kidnapped at the age of eight. Ripped away from the love and security of home.

Mariana adjusted her stride, trying to move in a fluid way, desperate not to cause some sudden jerk to her body that would cause a capsule to burst.

69

Remo began to struggle, hoping to wriggle free, but the men only gripped him tighter, delivering a couple of hard blows to his belly at the same time.

'Stay still!' one of the men commanded.

What's happening? What are they going to do to me?

He heard Leonardo laugh. A guttural, feral noise that lacked any sense of humanity.

Where am I? What's that grinding noise? And the smell . . . the animal stench of rotting flesh and decomposition.

The heat inside the hood was overpowering. Remo felt himself panting as he tried to suck air through the hessian.

'One . . . two . . . three.' Remo felt his body swinging to and fro as the men counted.

70

Wind Chill Factor is a scientifically recognized phenomenon which Riku and Takumi would have been wise to have learned a little about before their illegal bullet train excursion.

A human body operating in conditions of zero wind might be quite comfortable at five degrees Fahrenheit. But the effects of convection, and of evaporative cooling, mean that heat loss is directly related to the rate at which wind is moving across the surface of the skin.

A fifty kilometre an hour wind will effectively turn a five degree positive temperature into a figure of twenty-four degrees BELOW zero.

The two bullet train surfers had failed to realize this crucial dynamic; at speeds running at more than two hundred and fifty kilometres an hour they would be exposed to a wind chill factor that would be off the scale of human endurance.

Fifty or sixty degrees BELOW zero.

71

Nelson was still hunting for a cab, pacing up and down the taxi rank which was now empty. His thighs were pulsating with the agonizing pain of the coffee burn, and he felt himself on the verge of a full on stress attack.

He was kicking himself for not taking the drugs. They were still sitting, untouched, back up in his den.

'Can you believe these idiots?' he raged to a woman bystander. 'Leaving me to suffer like this? What is their problem?'

The woman gave him an awkward smile then quickly moved away from this slightly deranged looking individual.

'All I need is a goddam ride to the hospital!' he yelled at no one in particular.

He walked half a block, constantly scanning the street for a cruising cab. He thought about taking a bus but he had no idea what number would take him in the direction he needed. Then there was the subway, but he had always felt claustrophobic down there in the depths.

His iPhone rang; Paco on the line.

'I got another freeze-frame of those surfer dudes,' Paco told him. 'The train's really moving now!'

Nelson viewed the picture as he moved down the street, gutted he was having to experience this on a tiny screen and not on his four giant monitors at home.

'Post it on my blog,' he told Paco. He started to walk faster towards the hospital, muttering to himself as he went. People cleared a path in front of him, not wanting to meet his eye.

72

Remo crashed back to earth on a surface which was far from soft. Hard edges of metal tins and other junk were jabbing into his ribs, his legs. He twisted his head violently, trying to shrug off the hood, but it was tied tightly round his neck and he couldn't shift it.

He felt himself moving, heard the hum of motors close by. He tensed his wrists, trying desperately to free his hands.

Then the full horror of the situation overwhelmed him as he sussed where he was:

It was one of the city's municipal dumps. He was lying on a conveyor belt full of rubbish.

And that horrific clanking, thrashing noise was the flailing teeth of an industrial grinder at the end of the belt.

The pig-boy was about to be pulped.

73

HIDA MOUNTAIN RANGE, JAPAN

The professor looked down in horror.

The bear was hugging the main trunk of the cypress, shucking itself upwards in a series of determined moves.

It was incredibly strong, an expert climber.

The professor reached high above his head, desperately trying to catch hold of a higher branch to gain more height.

Yamada managed to clamber up a few more metres but then the branches were too thin to hold his weight and the bear was just below him and still rising.

He kicked out, smashing the bear on the muzzle, but it hardly seemed to notice the blow.

Instead the creature roared, shaking its huge head in fury and snapping at the professor's heels.

74

CITY SUBURBS, RIO DE JANEIRO, BRAZIL

Juliana threw the binoculars onto the backseat of the car and hit the accelerator hard. She cracked a handbrake turn, burning rubber as she fishtailed back down the hill towards the dump.

How much time did she have? Seconds rather than minutes.

Through gaps in the dump perimeter fence she got glimpses of the figure being swept along the belt. The kid was wriggling back and forwards but she knew there was no way he could escape.

She pulled a service revolver from the glovebox.

Her back-up still hadn't arrived but there was no time to lose now.

Juliana Amadeu raced at suicidal speed down the hill.

75

The train hit two hundred and fifty kilometres an hour, faster and faster as the surrounding countryside became nothing more than a blur.

'How are you doing?' Takumi yelled.

'Bad,' Riku shouted back.

Things were deteriorating with frightening speed for the two thrill seekers. The wind chill effect had pulled the temperature down to forty degrees below freezing.

Takumi could feel his very bones beginning to freeze.

When was the next station?

The boys hadn't even bothered to check.

76

HIDA MOUNTAIN RANGE, JAPAN

Canine teeth sliced at the professor. The bear was chewing on the sole of his leather hiking boots. If the creature pulled down now he would drag Yamada right out of the tree.

Then the bear reached up higher, splintering branches, clawing all the while. It began to try and snag the flesh on Yamada's calf.

His trousers ripped, he could feel the claws digging deeper into his muscle.

The entire tree was bending over at a crazy angle.

And still the bear was clawing at his feet.

'H . . . h . . . h . . . h-help me!' he screamed. But the woods were silent and the helicopter was no longer in earshot.

On the far side of the glade, Yamada could see his backpack.

77

The sound of the pulverizer was getting closer. The shrieking rip of rendering metal pulsed in the pig-boy's ears. Remo felt hot tears coursing down his cheeks. His wrists were almost breaking with the stress as he tried to pop the ties.

No go. He was trussed up like an oven ready turkey.

Remo felt wetness between his legs. He had lost control of his bladder in his terror. The heat was so intense inside the hood he felt he was being cooked alive.

He could hear Leonardo and the other men—chatting excitedly as they watched the show.

How could they stand there and watch him being crushed like a cockroach inside that infernal machine? Remo had no answer to that.

And still the conveyor belt moved along.

78

HIDA MOUNTAIN RANGE, JAPAN

Professor Yamada did the only thing he could do: he leapt out of the tree. It was a good four or five metre fall to the ground and he figured the soft grass and dead leaf litter at the base might break the fall.

He hit the ground with stunning force, his legs folding as the impact winded him.

In that moment his ankle broke.

He lay there for a few moments, wondering why he could feel no pain. Then he heard the bear slowly clambering back down the tree, its claws making a brittle scrabbling sound as they ripped into the bark.

'L . . . l . . . l . . . *l-leave me!*' he screamed.

He clawed at the earth, hurling stones and chunks of grass at the bear.

It dropped to the ground. And turned towards him.

79

WASTE INCINERATOR PLANT, RIO DE JANEIRO, BRAZIL

Sergeant Juliana Amadeu cracked a hard turn as she hit the entrance to the waste incinerator site. She screamed to a halt and primed the handgun.

Out of the vehicle. No time to even slam the door.

Leonardo and his guard clocked the cop car. They immediately ran for the Hummer.

No shots. They drove at high speed out of the yard.

Juliana wanted to stop them. But she had no time now. She was sprinting full throttle for the conveyor belt.

The trussed up figure now so close to obliteration.

She saw the site operators, standing dumbly by. She screamed: 'Police! Police! Stop the belt!'

The site operators ran for their office.

80

Takumi could see that his friend's lips were bright blue, that his cheeks and forehead were already scored a shade of black by frostbite.

He began to shiver—not the gentle shiver of the body trying to counter a chilly winter's day but the violent vibration of a system under severe assault.

The game had changed for them both. The question of remaining undetected was no longer important. The thing now was to survive.

'We have to try and stop the train,' Takumi yelled.

He began to kick his heel against the roof in the hope of attracting attention in the carriage below.

Would anybody hear them above the roar of the wheels on the track?

He had no idea. But he had to try.

81

HIDA MOUNTAIN RANGE, JAPAN

The professor managed to stand. Now his ankle *was* pulsing with a searing pain. It was unlike any he had experienced before.

The bear seemed to sense that the battle was nearly won.

Yamada started to stumble towards the edge of the glade, hopping in a grotesque fashion as the bear began to stalk him.

Get to the pack. Find the bottle. Defend yourself!

Seconds later he reached the undergrowth, fumbling for the pack as the bear advanced.

Open it! Fast. Undo the straps. Fingers shaking too much. Concentrate!

Where was the chemical? Yanmada reached inside and rummaged about, his heart trilling at what felt like a thousand beats a minute.

He felt the smooth touch of glass in his hand.

82

WASTE INCINERATOR PLANT, RIO DE JANEIRO, BRAZIL

Remo tried to roll. He figured he might flop off the conveyor belt if he could twist himself hard enough.

Blinded by the hood, he had no idea what he would fall *onto* but even a concrete floor was better than being crushed to death by those spinning tungsten teeth.

He arched his back and gave it a try, throwing his weight to his left and biting his cheek against the pain of the tins and sharp objects he was lying on.

No chance. The conveyor belt was running in a sort of channel, he realized. It had a hard rubber sidewall. He couldn't just roll off it.

He rolled back. Panting hard. The machine was now just metres away. He could feel the turbulent air it was kicking out.

Try again. Roll the other way. Try it to the right.

83

Takumi was still beating his feet and hands against the roof of the bullet train.

But the blows were feeble and he quickly realized that no one would hear them.

Why hadn't they brought warm clothes?

So dumb. They both had snowboarding gear at home.

Riku didn't even try to make a noise. He just snugged his head down in his arms, trying to get his face out of the wind blast.

Takumi cursed their stupidity. Why hadn't they figured out the danger? Any sense of exhilaration had been blown away. The invasive cold was Takumi's only preoccupation and he fervently wished that they had never had the crazy idea in the first place.

Takumi was starting to get it: this first great adventure could be their last.

84

HIDA MOUNTAIN RANGE, JAPAN

The bear swiped, striking Yamada with a paw the size of a dinner plate.

The bottle went flying. The professor fell onto his back, beating his hands in a futile gesture against the bear's torso for a couple of seconds before the animal lunged forward to bite him on the lower part of his face.

The bear got a grip on the professor's jaw.

There was a crunching sound as the bone rapidly splintered.

The professor could smell the fetid stink of the creature's breath, feel the surprising warmth of its mouth as it gnawed and ripped.

He reached out his hand. Found the bottle again.

The bear paused to chew on a morsel of flesh. Yamada twisted off the top of the bottle. Flung away the cap.

And threw the entire contents directly into the face of the bear.

85

Juliana dived forward, over the guard rail, the whole of her torso on the belt. She snatched the kid, both hands around his belly.

The tungsten teeth were a body length away. The noise and stench were unbearable.

She feared they were BOTH going to be ripped to pieces.

The cop gave a mighty snap of her arms, the muscles taut from years of Caproiera martial art training. An awkward move. Onto her knees. Then she was standing, facing the grinder, the kid half upright, held tight to her side.

Juliana flopped over the side rail and took the inert body of the kid with her. They both crashed onto the ground, and she felt her body crushed beneath his weight.

86

HIDA MOUNTAIN RANGE, JAPAN

The bear jerked back, a stunned grunt of surprise ripping from its throat as the irritant exploded around its head.

A mighty roar of pure rage followed as the creature pawed at its eyes.

It started to roll about the glade, whimpering in agony and beating at the side of its head.

Great clumps of soil were ripped up as the animal tried to fight off this unseen attacker.

Yamada knew he should move. The chemical had filled the air around him and its anaesthetizing effects were likely to knock him out.

But he wasn't fast enough. All the air seemed to be slammed out of his lungs as the cloud of formaldehyde vapour enveloped him.

Then he blacked out and the world went quiet.

87

Sergeant Juliana Amadeu unpicked the savage knots which bound the hood to Remo's neck. Then she gently removed it. Next, she loosened the cord around his wrists. The poor child was quivering like a tree in a gale, the terrifying ordeal still running in his mind.

She hugged him tight. 'You're OK. He's gone now.'

She was aware that they both stank like a couple of sewer rats.

In that moment two back-up cars turned into the yard.

'You two are under arrest,' she told the two site operators. 'Accomplices to attempted homicide.'

The men were handcuffed by her colleagues and she turned to Remo once more.

'Now. From the beginning. I think you'd better tell me what you've done to piss off Leonardo.'

88
SHINKANSEN BULLET TRAIN, EN-ROUTE NAGANO, JAPAN

Otto Krips, the unwitting German star of 'Rabid Rat bites Bullet Train dude' had no idea that he was becoming a global superstar. No idea that the clip featuring his painful—and embarrassing—rat encounter was fast becoming a YouTube favourite.

In fact he was feeling rather sorry for himself.

And also rather scared.

He had heard those two annoying American boys in the corner of the wagon joke that the rat had rabies. But what if that rat really *was* rabid? What if he got some exotic infection from the bite? He already felt a little feverish and queasy. And the bite had left his groin as sore as hell. Even the consoling words of his wife could do little to calm him down.

'Why don't you speak to the company doctor?' she suggested finally. 'Get some advice at least?'

Otto saw the sense in the idea. He worked for a big oil company in the States, had access to expert medical advice through the company quack. He could find out what injections he needed to get.

But a quick examination of his mobile revealed a problem. He had no number for the company medical department.

'Why don't you call Vincent?' his wife urged. 'He'll have the number.'

Vincent was the boss. An American oil tycoon who had become one of Otto's firmest and most trusted friends. In any case it would be good to tell him what had happened. Get some sympathy at least.

Otto selected the number on his mobile and activated the call.

89

WASTE INCINERATOR PLANT, RIO DE JANEIRO, BRAZIL

Juliana Amadeu got Remo safely into the back seat of her car and watched as the incinerator operators were loaded into a police van.

She was just about to quit the location when her sharp eyes noticed something.

An expensive leather jacket. Hanging on a post next to the office.

Could it belong to Leonardo? It certainly looked like something he would wear. In his desperation to get away he might have made a mistake and left it.

Reaching into the inside pocket, Juliana pulled out a small notepad. Bound in black leather, it was a classy looking item, with a slender silver pen held in a side sleeve.

She opened it up, hardly daring to hope.

What she saw was page after page of names, codes, and addresses. A big smile cracked her lips as she flipped through it; Leonardo's lifestyle was chaotic by most standards, but he was rigorous when it came to keeping records of his drug deals.

If they could decipher it, this was dynamite for the drug team.

Then she turned to the last page, finding the following information:

AZ 568 AT/SEA 1.5KG KENNY 978 37359 023

The first coded section seemed to be a flight number. Immediately she wondered if it was connected to a drug mule.

Anyway it was a good lead; she could investigate further back in the office.

90

It was mid afternoon local time when oil boss Vincent Bascombe got the call from his German colleague. He was in Hawaii on holiday, on a tourist boat, chugging slowly through choppy water as it rounded the southern point of the island of Nihue.

The boat trip was a special charter; Vincent and his wife Gena were touring the islands with their children and grandchildren to celebrate their fortieth wedding anniversary.

Money is no object when you own an oil company.

'Hi, Otto.' Vincent greeted his colleague warmly, 'How's it hanging?'

'"It" is not hanging so well,' came the bitter reply, 'I'm in Japan and I've been bitten by a rat.'

Vincent listened with sympathy to Otto's tale of woe, trying at the same time to keep a smile off his face. The thought of the rat dashing up his German friend's trousers was irresistibly funny.

'So I'm thinking of calling the company doc,' Otto concluded, 'and I need the number.'

'Hold the line,' Vincent told him. 'The number's in my PDA in the cabin.'

Vincent walked along the deck, seeing with pleasure that all fourteen family members were enjoying the cruise; sea lions were swimming playfully alongside the vessel, hoping for scraps. Seagulls were stationed just a few metres above the stern, also in the expectation of a free meal.

The captain would find a sheltered bay, they would open the champagne. Then the party would really begin.

91

THE MAYFIELD HOSPITAL, SEATTLE, USA

An exhausted and totally stressed out Nelson F. Muster made it to Mayfield Hospital.

He had jogged most of the way and was panting like an overheated dog.

He pushed his way into the bright neon interior of the hospital with some relief. It was getting difficult to walk as the blisters on his thighs had hardened up since the accident with the coffee and the pain was getting worse with every passing minute.

The waiting room was absolutely packed with casualty cases. Kids with cuts. People with fractured limbs. The bruised. The drunk. The concussed and the homeless who had simply come in to get out of the cold.

The admissions desk were fast and right on the case. Burns victims always got priority over broken limbs and other casualties as the speed of treatment is crucial to the recovery time of the patient.

Within two minutes he was taken to a cubicle where an efficient nurse applied silver nitrate cream to the burned parts of his thighs.

Then he was bandaged up and directed back to the waiting room until a consultant could see him.

By this stage Nelson was getting a pounding headache. He had always been prone to migraines—especially when he neglected to take his pills—and the stress of this unfortunate day had triggered one he already knew would be a monster.

He checked his mobile. Nothing from Paco. He flashed him a text asking for an update on the bullet train kids.

What was the latest? What was going on?

92

SHINKANSEN BULLET TRAIN, EN-ROUTE NAGANO, JAPAN

In the wiring cavity beneath the driver's compartment of the bullet train, Brad the rat was recovering from the gas attack.

He was still shaking with the fright of being chased but at least the searing pain in the little creature's eyes and lungs had diminished to the point of being bearable.

As he began to feel better, the rat checked out the immediate surroundings, finding that he was surrounded by cables of various sizes and shapes.

Now rats like to chew. It's in their nature to test out the texture and durability of just about every surface they come in contact with.

Brad sank his teeth into the rubber sleeve of one of the smaller cables. Beneath was bare copper, gleaming enticingly in the dim light which filtered into the hidden space.

Copper is a soft metal—much softer than the front incisors of a healthy rat which have a similar cutting strength to steel.

Brad nibbled through several cables in three minutes flat.

And with that, he cut through the main communications cable connecting the driver's cab to the aerial on the bullet train roof. From that moment on, the speeding train could not be contacted and the alarm systems to warn the driver of an electrical failure were now down.

The rat groomed himself for a while, then curled up in a ball and went to sleep.

93

Vincent reached his cabin and started to hunt for his PDA.

He was aware that Otto was holding on in Japan.

He checked his jacket pocket. No sign of it . . . maybe he had left it in his laptop case? Again, no sign.

Vincent picked up his overnight bag and unzipped it fast. As he did so, he accidentally knocked a bottle of chilled champagne off the table onto the floor.

The champagne bottle hit the deck with a heavy 'thud'. If the floor had been anything other than wooden decking it probably would have smashed itself to smithereens.

As it was, the bottle just impacted heavily, toppled over and rolled underneath the table.

'Clumsy!' Gena ticked off her husband.

'Sorry.' Vincent got down on his hands and knees to retrieve the bottle. He was relieved the thing hadn't exploded.

A moment later he had it back on the table where it belonged.

No damage had been done.

He found the PDA, got back on the phone and gave Otto the number for the company doctor.

'Good luck,' he told him.

And that ended the call.

Back in Rio, Juliana Amadeu was questioning Remo at the station. 'Tell me about the yard where Leonardo kept you. Can you take us back to that place?'

Remo shook his head. He had no idea where it was. The only clue he had seen was some graffiti on the gate in the shape of a dragon. But that was nothing like enough to lead the cop there. 'What else? Think hard. Any other clue?'

'There was a girl,' Remo suddenly blurted out, 'about eight years old. Kidnapped and held in the cell next to mine.'

That was when Juliana became a lot more interested.

She started to interrogate Remo in more detail. Then she remembered that flight code in Leonardo's notebook, her logical mind piecing it together.

Leonardo had kidnapped a young girl. He was almost certainly holding her as hostage for a drug mule operation. And that 1.5kg note was a dead giveaway.

Juliana briefed her colleagues and they began to search the database. Quickly, they found it. An eye-witness—a well-meaning neighbour—had filed a report of an abduction of a young girl named Ester. 'The family name is Martinez,' she was told, 'and she's eight years old. It happened two days ago.'

Juliana thought fast. 'Now we need to find out if there's a member of that girl's family on that flight. There's no time to lose.'

The cop clicked on to Amadeus.net, the international portal for flight information. She quickly discovered that the flight mentioned in Leonardo's notepad had just landed at Seattle.

From now on, every second would count.

95

NIHUE ISLAND, HAWAII, PACIFIC OCEAN

Vincent and his family had gathered on the deck. They were loaded down with presents, cards, and all the goodies they needed for a serious celebration. Two cooks and an assistant were preparing smoked salmon blinis and fresh fish in the boat's galley.

Gena gave her present first.

It was a watch. A gold Rolex GMT Timemaster with a lapis blue face and a ring of finely cut diamonds embedded into the bezel. Vincent was delighted; it's not every day that a man gets to receive a timepiece worth more than thirty thousand dollars.

Vincent removed the watch carefully from the snug velvet caress of the presentation case. He held it up to the light for a few seconds as the family crowded around, awe-struck at the sheer quantity of gold and diamonds the piece incorporated.

There was no doubt about it, it was a watch fit for a king.

Vincent tried to slip the watch on his wrist, but quickly found a snag. The bracelet (eighteen carat gold, just like the watch itself) was way too big for him.

'Have to get it altered, I guess,' he said with a little sigh.

'I'll take it in for you the moment we get back home,' Gena told him, quietly admonishing herself for neglecting to adjust the bracelet before the cruise.

'No problem.' Vincent gave his wife a consoling little kiss on the cheek and picked up the champagne bottle.

'Let's have a drink, shall we?' He pulled off the foil wrapping from the neck and twisted the wire seal.

96

SHINKANSEN BULLET TRAIN, EN-ROUTE NAGANO, JAPAN

Saki had returned to her seat on the strict instructions of the train steward. Now she sat with the empty cage of her pet rat on her knees, sniffling in a sulk as a potent mix of grief and anger bubbled away inside her.

She had done her best. She had begged, pleaded with the train officials not to kill her rat. It wasn't her fault that Brad had escaped, she told them, and really he didn't mean any harm. If they would just let her call his name again she was sure that . . .

But no one had listened. They had raged about fleas and bacteria and other ridiculous accusations, held her back from the scene and threatened that she would be thrown off the train if she continued to protest.

Now, the fumigation team had done their dirty work and her beloved Brad was even now lying poisoned and dying somewhere in the kitchen of the train.

Or was he?

A sudden glimmer of hope filled Saki with new resolution. Brad was a survivor. He had been lost several times before and had always lived to tell the tale. Once he had been stuck below the floorboards in her father's flat for a week and he had eventually come out with nothing more than a raging thirst.

She resolved to at least go and have a final look.

There were five customs officers in the duty room at Seattle international airport when the call came in from Rio.

Juliana was passed to Juan Cortes, a thirty-five-year-old inspector who had just started his shift. Cortes was a conscientious guy, had worked his way up through the ranks of the Washington State Customs service in a fifteen year career track that had won him several commendations.

'How can I help you, sergeant?' he asked Juliana after a few pleasantries had been exchanged.

'We have some intelligence to share,' Juliana told him. 'We believe there's a courier on flight AZ 568 coming in from Atlanta. Her name is Mariana Martinez. Brazilian passport. She's eighteen years old, dark hair, travelling alone. That's all the information we have at this point.'

Cortes hit the keypad, bringing up a flight arrivals schedule within seconds.

'The baggage is being unloaded now,' he told Juliana. 'The passengers will be picking it up soon.'

'Then you'd better get down there fast,' the Brazilian cop told him with some urgency.

Cortes thanked her and cut the call. He quit the office and hurried down the corridor. The call had certainly livened up the shift and he felt his heart rate rise as he rushed towards the baggage reclaim area.

There wasn't much to go on. There might be many dark haired girls travelling solo on that flight.

And she might even now be passing through the customs point. He picked up his pace, breaking into a jog.

98

As soon as Vincent Bascombe loosened the wire seal, the cork exploded from the chilled bottle of champagne.

The incident where the bottle had been knocked off the table had shaken up the contents with a violent shock.

As a result, as Vincent eased open the seal, the cork exploded out a fraction of a second *sooner* than he had anticipated. The consequence was that the bottle wasn't *quite* pointing the way he had planned as the cork erupted.

'Whoaaa!' he laughed.

The cork shot into the air, bounced off a metal stanchion holding a lifeboat in place, then smacked straight into the eye of his sixteen-year-old granddaughter Mia.

'Ow!!'

Mia let out a yell of pain, her hand jerking up in a reflex action to cover the eye.

'Oh, Vincent,' Gena admonished him, 'you really should take more care.'

The family left their seats, gathered tightly around Mia in the entrance to the cabin. She was making a brave face of it but it had obviously hurt like crazy.

'It's OK,' she told her grandfather, 'just a bit of a bruise, that's all.'

99

INTERNATIONAL AIRPORT, SEATTLE, USA

At Seattle international airport Inspector Juan Cortes was watching the baggage reclaim like a hawk.

The hunt was on. The call from Rio had put an exciting twist on the shift.

He spotted one possible suspect straight away. A pretty young Latino girl in her late teens. She was picking at her nails and there was a thin sheen of sweat on her top lip. Both a real giveaway.

He couldn't be a hundred per cent certain but this target looked like a good bet.

He moved back into the inspection area as the young passenger picked up her suitcase. She walked slightly unsteadily through the 'nothing to declare' entry point, her eyes shifting from side to side as she scanned the officers.

Cortes stepped out in front of her, a move that caused a flash of panic to cross her face.

'Where are you travelling from?' Cortes asked her.

'Atlanta.'

'Can I see your ticket?'

'OK.'

Mariana's hands were shaking as she handed him the ticket. He flipped through it.

OK, she'd just flown from Atlanta, but she'd begun her journey in Rio.

And the name on the ticket was the same one that the Rio contact had given him.

Result. This was the mule.

100
ROOF OF BULLET TRAIN, EN-ROUTE NAGANO, JAPAN

Takumi could no longer feel his feet inside his trainers.

His core body temperature was getting terrifyingly close to the point where vital functions would begin to fail. His eyes were almost completely frozen shut; Riku was just a blurred mirage on the other side of the roof, huddled in mute misery. The landscape was flashing past in a continuous blur.

Takumi felt a black cloud engulfing him. His vision seemed to be tunnelling down to a pinprick of light as the immense cold caused his brain to shut down. He tried desperately to stay conscious but the cold had gone too deep.

A great wave of self-pity engulfed him.

All they had wanted was to get some thrills.

It was just supposed to be a game.

Then, bizarrely, he felt a brief surge of warmth inside him. The sensation of comforting heat wrapped him like a blanket.

He could not know that this is one of the deadliest indicators of serious hypothermia, a final twist in the fast deterioration which comes with extreme cold.

'It's getting warmer!' he yelled at Riku. But his friend made no response.

The glow felt real. So much so that he felt the shivering cease.

Takumi felt a big smile crack across his face.

The frozen blue flesh of his lips ripped as he grinned but he didn't feel it at all.

101
INTERNATIONAL AIRPORT, SEATTLE, USA

Customs Inspector Cortes fixed the young Latino girl with a probing look as he searched her bag. 'So, you began your journey in Rio, right?'

'Yes. I live there.'

'You look uncomfortable,' Cortes told her. 'Are you sure you're not sick?'

Mariana forced a bright smile even though her belly was killing her. 'No. Really I'm feeling fine. Just tired after the trip.'

'Uh huh. And what are you planning to do in Seattle?'

'Oh, I'm just going to spend a week with my boyfriend.'

'OK. What's his name?'

And there it was. That millisecond of hesitation as Mariana tried to remember the name she had been given. 'John . . . Johnny.'

She was lying.

'Have you ever heard of what is commonly called a drug mule, Mariana?'

'Yes. I guess so . . .'

'Mostly it's cocaine. Sometimes in a hidden compartment in a case, and other times the mule swallows the drug in rubber capsules. The second way is very dangerous, Mariana, if a package bursts it's a seriously bad way to die.'

Mariana stared at the floor, fighting back tears.

'Would you agree to have an X-ray so we can check this out?'

102

The seagull was a regular old yellow-legged gull, the ugly great bruiser of a bird that is common the world over. This gull had been following the Bascombe's boat for an hour or more and it was hungry as hell.

Now, something caught the bird's attention.

There was a shiny object on the table at the back of the boat.

To the gull's voracious eye it looked like the shimmering, glittering scales of a fish.

What was more, the humans had moved away, creating an opportunity. The bird tucked in its wings, going into a short and expert dive.

The seagull snatched up the watch in its beak and jumped off the table with wings outstretched.

'Hey!' Gena Bascombe lunged towards the back of the boat, flapping her arms to try and scare the bird away. 'He's got the watch!' she yelled.

Vincent made a dash for the bird. The grandchildren screamed excitedly. A crew member picked up a boathook and raised it to strike a blow.

The gull squawked in alarm as the crew member swung the boathook through the air. He missed the bird by just a few centimetres as it banked abruptly to the side.

The gull had had enough of this attack—and the strange shiny thing didn't feel like the fish it had seemed to be; it opened its beak.

The watch plunged into the sea in a brilliant flash of gold and diamonds.

The helicopter crew were just about ready to give up on their search for the missing academic and his bear stalker when they received a radio call from base.

'MR806 . . . MR806 copy. Status report please.'

'No sign of the missing man. We've searched five square kilometres on the east side of the range but no warning fire or ground markings.'

'OK. We have a new request for you. There's some viral internet thing going on about a couple of kids surfing on a bullet train.'

Some smart cookie at the Nagano Police Mountain Rescue Unit had put two and two together. They had taken a look at the map and realized that they had a helicopter right in the zone that the bullet train would shortly be moving through.

'How close are you to the Tokyo–Nagano railway line?'

'Five minutes,' Akiba told them.

'There's a Nagano-bound bullet train due to pass close by you shortly. There's rumoured to be two kids on the roof. Can you check it out and report back?'

The pilot and co-pilot looked at each other in amazement.

'Why don't they just stop the train?' the pilot asked.

'They've got some sort of comms problem. They can't contact the train on their radio loop.'

'OK. We'll go and take a look,' the pilot confirmed. The crew put the EC135 into a steep turn, heading for the train track.

104

Mariana chewed her fingers as she thought furiously; what had the cartel told her if she was threatened with an X-ray? Ah yes. 'I'm pregnant,' she told her interrogator.

'Any objections to taking a simple pregnancy test?' Cortes immediately countered. 'It only takes a couple of minutes.'

'Well, erm . . .' Mariana's mind was blank with panic.

A few minutes later a female officer led Mariana to a toilet cubicle and handed her a urine test kit. Step by step, the net was closing in.

The test took just a couple of minutes to reveal the truth and Inspector Cortes had the girl brought back to his office.

'So you lied to us about being pregnant.' Cortes opened with a harsh line of attack.

Mariana stared at the floor as tears filled her eyes. She felt a terrible wave of shame overwhelm her—she hated to lie under any circumstances.

'Things . . . must have changed,' she said, but without much hope he would believe it.

Cortes adopted a more reasonable tone. 'Listen, Mariana. You see, what happens sometimes is that girls get *forced* into acting as drug couriers. You might find we are more sympathetic if that is the case. But you'd have to tell us the names of the people who have done this.'

The girl said nothing.

'OK. I'm going to arrange for you to have an X-ray. I believe you are carrying drugs internally and I want to check it out.'

105

Out on the Hawaiian island of Nihue the Bascombe family wedding anniversary celebration had run out of fizz. Even the champagne had gone flat.

The lost Rolex had soured what had promised to be a very special day.

'Maybe we can see it lying on the bottom?' someone suggested.

A couple of them put on snorkelling goggles then leant over the side of the boat. But the water was too deep to see the bottom. The watch had vanished into the depths.

Then Vincent got a brainwave: 'You got any diving gear on board?' he asked the captain.

'We got two sets. We keep them charged in case we get a problem with a propellor.'

Vincent nodded. 'And how deep is this water?'

'We put out about twenty metres of anchor chain.'

'Twenty metres, huh? I could go down and look for that watch myself.'

Sixteen-year-old Mia clapped her hands. 'Fantastic idea! Can I dive with you? Please?'

'You don't have much experience . . .' her mother said.

'Pretty please.' Mia fixed her parents with a pleading look.

'Of course you can dive with me!' Vincent exclaimed. 'Cheer you up after that damn cork hit you in the eye. We're not leaving this place until Mia and I have that watch safe back on board!'

106

Nelson sat there in the waiting room for a bit, chewing his nails with frustration. His thighs were still smarting like hell but he hardly noticed the pain, he was so fixated on those bullet train guys.

Then, in the corner of the waiting room he saw an office door. It was slightly open, open enough that he could see a computer sitting on a desk inside.

Nelson found himself wondering. Would it have an internet connection? He figured it would. Pretty much every terminal in the world was online these days.

Hmmmm. Nelson saw a possibility opening up.

Then he felt his mobile vibrate as a text came through.

Paco. An update.

'The bullet train just got captured by another station webcam. The dudes still surfing on the roof!'

Nelson felt sick. He was missing all the action.

He looked round the waiting room, checking to see if there was a security guard. There. Over by the water fountain. A uniformed man with a belt full of gadgets and a long wooden cosh hanging down his side.

Nelson watched as the man crossed to the reception desk and struck up a half-hearted conversation with a nurse.

Nelson took his chance. He rose from his seat and walked across to the office.

He closed the door quietly behind him and crossed to the desk. The computer was on standby. He clicked on the mouse, enjoying the reassuring sound of the machine booting up as he waited.

107

Customs Inspector Cortes made the arrangements with a couple of calls to the local health authority.

'Come on.' Cortes took Mariana firmly by the arm. 'We're going down town to take an X-ray.'

Cortes escorted the Brazilian girl to the customs vehicle which had been brought around to the loading bay outside the terminal.

Seattle Airport is not a big enough drug portal to justify the cost of a dedicated medical X-ray facility. Suspected traffickers are taken to one of several local hospitals in town, depending on availability of a machine.

Cortes put Mariana in the back of the vehicle, took his place in the driver's seat and drove out of the airport complex. A few minutes later he was filtering into the heavy traffic on the Interstate Five which would take them north and into the city itself.

Mariana had figured she might be handcuffed or somehow restrained in the back of the customs car, but actually her hands were completely free.

When the suspect is a male it is normal for an armed guard to go with them in the back of the vehicle. Normally they are handcuffed as well. But with female suspects the rules tend to be a bit more relaxed and Mariana had given Cortes no indication that she might try to escape.

But that didn't mean she wasn't up for giving it a try if she got the chance.

What were the alternatives?

Years in an American prison. And God only knew what fate for her sister.

108

As the bullet train reached maximum speed, Riku began to have strange visions. The life-threatening cold was causing him to hallucinate.

At first he thought he was falling out of an aeroplane. The mountains rushing past the train were the ground coming up to meet him. Then he dreamt he was on a beach, with waves crashing against his body.

The sensation of cold had gone—his body was now so frozen there was no sensation of pain at all.

And still the train kept surging forward, penetrating through tunnels and valleys as it skirted the Hida mountain range.

Then, the final episode of this young thrill seeker's life.

Riku tried to *stand*.

The young thrill seeker was totally blind, hallucinating, living out some weird dream. In his mind he was standing on the edge of a cliff, and all he could think about was getting away from the edge.

He grabbed hold of the pantograph struts, pulled himself up with grim determination. He straightened his legs, feeling the muscles crack as they stretched.

He felt out of his own body, a spectator at the scene.

He forced his body up against the incredible wind rush.

109

MAYFIELD HOSPITAL, SEATTLE, USA

Nelson had the computer up and running. He opened up his Skype account and immediately got hold of Paco. 'You are missing some serious stuff,' Paco told him. 'The kids aren't moving. Like they're frozen or something. I got two more webcam shots and they're looking like they're in trouble.'

'What?'

Nelson went to Gmail and frantically punched in the password for his account; five seconds after that he had Paco's freeze-frame right in front of him.

He studied the picture intently, zooming in by using the control wheel of the mouse. Paco was right. Both of the Japanese kids were lying in weird positions. Maybe they'd been electrocuted?

Then he heard the door open behind him.

'Hey!' The guard's voice was immediately aggressive. 'What do you think you're doing here?'

Nelson whipped round as he heard the voice.

'This room is private,' said the guard. 'I need you to return to the waiting area straight away.'

Nelson gave the guard an angry stare.

'Just give me a minute, will you? I'm almost done.'

The guard grabbed Nelson by the shoulder. Nelson shrugged him off and pushed him away with an open hand. 'I said get out of my face!'

The guard reached into his belt. He brought out his taser and aimed the stun gun directly at the raging patient in front of him.

'I'm counting to ten now and you leave this room. If not, you get tasered. One, two, three, four . . .'

110

SHINKANSEN BULLET TRAIN, EN-ROUTE NAGANO, JAPAN

Saki walked quickly through carriages four and three and entered the final carriage before the catering wagon.

She knew she would have to be cautious now as the chief steward had already warned her there would be someone on guard to prevent passengers accidentally entering the fumigated area.

There he was: a huge and stern looking guard at the doorway.

Saki walked confidently along the passenger aisle, heading for some empty seats in the middle of the carriage. She could now see the sliding door behind the guard; it had been sealed off with some red and white tape marked with the words 'Do not cross'.

She took a quick look around her; the nearby passengers were not paying her any attention at all. One man was asleep with his newspaper on his chest, and two elderly women were chatting to each other in an animated fashion.

There were a few loud tourists sitting nearby but they were busy taking pictures out of the window.

Saki took a seat and pretended to read a discarded celebrity magazine.

She would have to wait her chance to sneak past the guard.

Hang on in there, Brad, she thought, I'm coming for you.

111

Mia Bascombe stripped down to her underwear and pulled on the one-piece neoprene wetsuit. She was thrilled at this opportunity to dive with her grandfather even if the nerves were already running.

She had only dived twice before. And never so deep as this.

'What do you think, kids?' Vincent pulled on his wet-suit and struck a tongue-in-cheek strong man pose for his grandchildren. He looked like a beached whale.

'Go, Gramps! Go, Mia!' The younger kids were jumping around with excitement at this unexpected diversion.

Mia picked up a weight belt and slipped it around her waist.

'This is dangerous, Vince. Mia's a beginner and you haven't dived for years,' his wife told him.

'No problem,' Vincent replied, 'I'll be right by her side. She won't come to any harm.'

The two of them shrugged on their stab jackets and air bottles, snapped the plastic fins onto their feet.

'I don't know.' Gena was close to tears.

'Don't fuss, honey. Mia'll be fine. We'll find that watch if it's the last thing we do.'

So saying, Vincent Bascombe snapped his goggles onto his face and adjusted them so the fit was tight against his skin. Moments later Mia did the same.

Then they both peeled off backwards into the sparkling blue waters of the Pacific.

112

Remo the pig-boy was back on the streets.

The questioning had finished. The police had let him go.

Now he walked through the dark alleyways of the *favela*, heading for the rubbish pile where he had left his backpack of pigswill.

He kept to the deepest shadows, terrified he might run into Leonardo and his son. But mostly he was thinking about the girl. The kidnapped one: Ester. The raw edge of her fear had seeped inside him and he couldn't shake it off.

He stopped to drink from a tap, relishing the cold bite of the fresh water and splashing some of it on the back of his neck.

What were they planning to do with her, he wondered? He shivered. He was old enough to understand how terrible her fate could be.

The questions buzzed around his head as he trudged through the slum, keeping his ears alert for the roar of the drug lord's Hummer.

If only he could have done something to help her.

But now the chance was lost.

Or was it? If he could only find that compound then he could tell the police where she was.

She might still survive.

Remo made a decision. There were many hours of darkness left. He was bone tired but he couldn't let that girl down. He would walk the streets, looking for the compound. It was the least he could do.

113

The EC135 search and rescue helicopter skimmed low over a jagged mountain pass. The green valley that opened up to them contained the bullet train track.

'There it is,' the pilot exclaimed.

They were bang on time. The Nagano-bound bullet train came speeding out of a tunnel on the far side of the valley.

The co-pilot pushed down the nose and banked in at an acute angle until the EC135 was where he wanted it. The helicopter was now flying just a few metres above the speeding bullet train, positioned about one rotor's length to the side.

'OK. We have visual,' the pilot confirmed into his radio. 'And we can see two kids on the top of the train.'

'What is their condition? Over.'

The heli nudged even closer as the pilots tried to get a closer look at the kids.

'OK. One of these kids is definitely unconscious and the other is trying to stand up.'

The pilot made small adjustments to the collective as the heli was buffeted by the powerful slipstream of turbulence the bullet train kicked up.

'He's trying to stand up? What the hell is he doing?'

'No idea. He's holding on to one of the power units. His face and hands are pretty blue.'

'Roger that. Stand by for further instructions.'

114

In a dirty drinking shack at the top end of the *favela*, drug baron Leonardo was waiting for a call from the USA.

He was in a foul mood; the incident at the dump had been the closest he had ever come to being arrested.

Now he checked his watch for the umpteenth time. *Why hadn't he had the call?*

The mule's plane had landed in Seattle. He'd checked the online information board for the airport and ascertained that much. Then add, say, twenty minutes for the plane to taxi to the terminal. Then add, say, another thirty minutes for the girl to pick up her bag from the carousel.

He should have got the call ages ago to say she was safely through customs.

But he'd heard nothing.

What was happening?

Had the girl been busted?

'Bring the sister here,' he told one of his guards. 'This is not looking good.'

115

Riku straightened up to his full height.

In that moment his head brushed against the live electric cable feeding the train with current.

Twenty-five thousand volts zapped through his body as he jerked and spasmed with the shock.

The top of his skull melted with the extreme heat generated by the current. His brains were instantly liquidized to a boiling mash of tissue and his legs kicked out in a series of grotesque kicks as his arms cartwheeled uncontrollably.

He spun, then toppled forward, his legs kicking out as he was blown down the roof.

Riku's body smashed into pantograph number seven, the impact buckling the support struts and ripping three of the four securing bolts out of the roof.

The broken pantograph fell away from the electric cable and began to smash up and down against the roof as the air current buffeted it.

The event went unrecorded in the cab of the train. The cables which might have alerted the driver had been severed by Brad the rat and the motor system was designed so that the other pantographs automatically sucked up more power to compensate.

A single bolt was holding the damaged strut in place.

116

The guard braced himself to fire.

If he squeezed the taser trigger now, compressed nitrogen would send the two probes shooting through the air towards their target. The barbed probes would embed in skin or clothing, then fifty thousand volts of electricity would be sent down the high voltage cables.

Nelson would be rendered helpless. A quivering wreck on the floor as his muscles contracted in agonizing waves of pain.

'Sir. Your final warning.'

That was when Nelson flipped. He just lost the plot completely.

The agonizing burns. The drilling pain of the headache. The missed medication. The overwhelming, gut-wrenching vexation of having to miss all that extraordinary action in Japan with the bullet train. This violent guard with his weapons and his threats.

Nelson F. Muster picked up the computer terminal and hoisted it bodily off the desk. The power cables ripped from the wall with the sheer force of the action.

'You want me to get off the frickin' computer?' he yelled at the security guard. 'I'll get off the frickin' computer like this, OK?'

Then with a roar of pure rage, Nelson F. Muster threw the computer out of the open window and down into the street below.

117

HIDA MOUNTAIN RANGE, JAPAN

Professor Yamada came round with a start.

The effects of the formaldehyde had worn off.

There was no sign of the bear.

He stared into the forest but there was no sound of any big creature moving around. He realized that the chemical must have worked—stung the creature into a retreat.

He turned on his side so that his undamaged leg was in contact with the ground. His head was aching severely but the wounds had stopped bleeding. He began to pull himself across the clearing. Ahead was a rise in the terrain.

He put in an extra effort with his arms, managed to pull himself up the bank. As he reached it the professor found he could look down into the valley below. At the bottom he could see the jade waters of the lake, with the metallic rails of the bullet train tracks snaking round in an elegant curve.

Then he saw a dark rectangular outline against the grass. It was a shack.

Professor Yamada guessed the shack was a railway workers' shed. There might be a blanket there—or even a heater. Maybe even a telephone connection to a control room somewhere.

It was a long way down. Could he make it?

118

NIHUE ISLAND, HAWAII, PACIFIC OCEAN

The water was colder than Mia had expected. *Much* colder. The wetsuit was thinner than she would have liked and she instantly felt her skin pucker up into goosepimples.

Right from the beginning of the dive, she didn't feel right. She didn't have enough weight round her waist, she was too buoyant; as a result she had to fight a bit too hard to get down, kicking strenuously with her fins but making little headway.

Her grandfather seemed perfectly at ease with his gear, finning rapidly into the deep.

Mia's mask didn't fit very well. Her eye was still hurting from the champagne cork. A trickle of seawater had already entered, slopping around the bottom of the mask in an irritating way.

The regulator giving her air was also not right for the size of her mouth, so that she was continually having to blow the salt water out of the airline.

She should have thought longer and harder about making this crazy dive.

Under different circumstances she might have resurfaced and scrubbed the whole idea. But all the family were up there on the boat, willing them both to find the watch. She couldn't quit now, not without looking like an idiot.

Then she saw the anchor chain.

That would be a way to get down to the seabed.

Mia gripped it, pulling herself bodily down into the depths.

119

PARK STREET, SEATTLE, USA

The computer screen was an old-fashioned one with a cathode ray tube. It weighed about seven kilogrammes. Enough to punch its way right through the windscreen of the Ford Crown Victoria police vehicle which was crawling through heavy traffic in the street below.

Inspector Cortes yelped in surprise as the glass caved in next to him, the heavy computer falling right into the passenger seat as the pieces of glass showered his hands and legs. His passenger—the Brazilian girl in the back—curled up to protect herself.

Cortes's first thought was that the vehicle was somehow being attacked. The girl sitting in the back could have a belly full of some gangster's cocaine and someone might be crazy enough to try and rescue her before it was lost.

Could he have been followed from the airport?

He climbed from the vehicle, immediately reaching into his duty belt for his Smith and Wesson handgun. Cortes quickly scanned the street. He saw no further threat.

He looked up, saw an open window but no movement.

Strange.

Very strange.

120

The pilots had watched in horror as the boy had fallen. Then they spotted the broken pantograph. The metal structure was banging up and down like crazy, still attached to the roof by a single bolt.

'There's something wrong with the power supply,' he told his fellow pilot through the comms. 'That unit looks loose. Let's get in tighter so we can see what's happening.'

The heli repositioned relative to the train, shifting so that it was flying level to the pantograph. They were close enough to see the sparks which were flying intermittently from the electrical conductor as it nudged against the live cable above it.

'Heli to base,' he radioed, 'one of the kids has fallen against a metal conductor and broken it. The train is definitely damaged.'

'Roger that. Stand by for further instructions.'

'Wilco.'

The helicopter maintained position.

121

Nelson F. Muster rushed at the security guard like a charging bull. His body slammed into the man in a raging wall of muscle and fat. That was when the inexperienced and poorly trained security guard discovered—as he pulled the trigger—that he hadn't flicked off the safety catch on the taser stun gun.

The taser rattled to the floor—and so did the guard. He was winded, gasping for air as his thorax heaved in and out.

Nelson picked up the taser and put it in his pocket. Then he crossed to the other side of the room where there was a second computer terminal. He switched it on, tapping his fingers against the desk impatiently as it booted up.

Click. Internet Explorer. Back online. Now to check out what was happening with that bullet train.

As soon as he accessed his trainspotter website he saw to his amazement that one hundred and thirty thousand people were online.

One hundred and thirty thousand!

Nelson got a serious hit of pleasure out of that. Those people were on the site because *his* eagle eye had spotted the two dudes on that webcam. That's the type of thing that makes people like Nelson happy.

'Hey, Paco. Me again. Have you *seen* how many people we've got online right now? Think we can go for a million hits an hour?'

'Sure, buddy! Let's link in to some more sites.'

Nelson was distracted by a moan from the corner of the room. 'I'm in Dr Sota's room,' the guard gasped into his walkie-talkie, 'urgent backup required.'

122

NIHUE ISLAND, HAWAII, PACIFIC OCEAN

Mia pulled herself down the anchor chain. Deeper and deeper, pulling arm over arm and kicking her fins in a constant scissor movement. Finally, after a bigger struggle than she could have imagined, the young girl reached the sea floor where she paused to take stock of the situation.

Gradually her vision adjusted to the low light. She began to pick out movement—the sensual swaying of seaweed which covered the floor, the shadowy shapes of some quite large fish—groupers, she thought, or maybe even tuna, which were moving in tight circles around her position.

There was a small canyon cut into the sea floor, some dark shadows that looked like sea caves.

Her grandfather appeared out of the gloom, gave her the universal 'all OK' hand signal and a smile.

There was no sign of the watch. In fact the seaweed was really dense and Mia knew instinctively that was going to make the search more than a little complicated.

They would have to rummage through the fronds with their bare hands.

They would just have to hope that there were no poisonous scorpion fishes or hungry moray eels hiding in there.

Mia Bascombe let go of the anchor chain and finned after her grandfather, swimming towards the area where they imagined the watch might have fallen.

Mia checked her air gauge. Her strenuous descent had already cost her twenty per cent of her air.

123

PARK STREET, SEATTLE, USA

Mariana had absolutely no idea what had caused the windscreen to shatter and even less idea why a computer should be sitting in the passenger seat of the vehicle. But she did know that the customs officer was distracted now, out of the vehicle, and that an opportunity had opened up for her.

This was her chance.

A chance to escape.

She had nothing to lose. An X-ray would reveal the drugs, destroy her life—and that of her little sister—for ever.

Mariana tried the door release. No dice. It was kiddy locked to prevent an easy escape.

Don't give up. This might be the only opportunity you get.

Go for it. He's still not looking!

Mariana quickly slipped into the front of the vehicle, making the awkward manoeuvre with her eyes fixed on the customs guy—still standing a short distance away. He was engaged in conversation with someone standing near the vehicle.

Mariana pushed the computer aside and, holding her breath, she released the door catch on the passenger side. She quietly stepped out of the vehicle, then moved swiftly away.

She saw a shopping precinct just half a block away.

She ran for it.

Some seconds later she heard the cry of alarm behind her as the customs guy realized what was happening.

124

On the bullet train roof, Takumi felt so hot that he would have ripped off his T-shirt if his frozen fingers could have performed the task.

He had no way of knowing that the sensation of bodily heat was completely false—induced by freezing damage to the hypothalamus, the gland which regulates body temperature.

Dying mountaineers have occasionally been reported to experience the same effect: wanting to remove clothes when their bodies are racked with hypothermia. Some are found almost naked.

Takumi's warmth was an illusion and it soon faded. It was quickly replaced once more by the probing, remorseless, freezing wind.

Takumi curled his fingers round the base of the pantograph as the wind continued its efforts to rip him off the train. The metal was so cold that his flesh stuck to it immediately.

He didn't even register the helicopter which was flying alongside.

He felt the world beginning to fade out, his brain shutting down as exposure and hypothermia took him one more step towards oblivion.

125

Mariana ran as fast as she could into the precinct. Her belly was feeling mighty messed up with all those plastic capsules jiggling around but she could stand the pain if it meant getting away.

She thanked her lucky stars she was wearing trainers.

There were a dozen or so stores arranged around a paved courtyard. She ducked into the second store. It was stacked with mattresses and bed linen and the sales staff were distracted at the back of the shop. Mariana found a gap between two mattresses which were stacked upright.

She wriggled in. Then risked a quick look out through a small gap.

There he was. The customs guy ran into the square—then paused in the middle of the precinct as he looked around.

Seeing no sign of Mariana, he entered the mall and disappeared inside.

Mariana left the store and ran down the street away from the mall. She saw a rank of payphones and headed for them immediately. She slammed in some coins and dialled the number from memory.

'Yes.' A man's voice. Local. An American, not Hispanic.

'This is Carnival.' Mariana gave her password. She heard a loud exhalation of air. Whoever was on the other end was mightily relieved to get this call.

'OK. Where are you?' Mariana explained the locale—naming several of the shops she could see.

'Don't move. I'm coming to get you.'

126

Leonardo was sitting with his fellow gang members in the Parada de Lucas slum when the call came through on his mobile.

Kenny. At last some news from Seattle.

'I got the call from the mule. I'm picking her up now.'

Leonardo silently punched the air with sheer relief.

'What was the delay? I've been waiting for an hour, going crazy here.'

'Not my fault, man. The mule didn't call me from the airport.'

'Why not? She get stopped by customs?'

'I dunno. Anyway I'm picking her up now and I'll take her to my place.'

'Call me back as soon as you have the merchandise.'

'OK, buddy. Speak later.'

Leonardo's prayers had been answered. He raised a bottle to his mouth and drank a deep swig of beer to celebrate.

Then he thought of the young girl he had captive.

By rights he should set her free now the mule had done her job. But the night had been a bad one and he was still in a sour mood.

He was inclined to kill her.

Leonardo had always hated loose ends.

127

On the roof of the Shinkansen bullet train, Takumi was just a few degrees away from fade out. His pulse and respiration rates had fallen way below levels at which he could function. His cellular metabolic functions were closing down one by one.

Now, he began to exhibit a well-documented symptom of hypothermia known as terminal burrowing; an irrational belief that safety—and warmth—can be attained by burrowing like an animal away from the cold.

In Takumi's case this meant that he unfurled his grip from the support tower of pantograph number six and started to try and claw his way into a narrow two centimetre wide gap in the mounting plate it was sitting on.

This manic and totally desperate action left him un-anchored in the savage wind. As he broke his nails in the frantic scrabble for protection he felt his body begin to move.

Cortes ran through the mall, searching the aisles as he went.

No sign of the girl. She seemed to have vanished.

Cortes thought rapidly. What would he do in her situation? He had to figure that she wasn't familiar with the city. His mind sorted through the options.

A telephone. She would have to reach her contact.

Cortes thought about the neighbourhood. There were telephones a couple of blocks away. She might have dodged back.

He hurried back out of the mall, reaching the spot one minute later. There. A row of five public telephones on a corner.

Yes! There she was. Cortes felt a surge of relief as he saw the girl lurking in a shadowy alley near the phones.

What would she do now?

Cortes dropped back into the doorway of a shoeshop, putting himself out of Mariana's eyeline and watching her reflection in the glass.

The girl was waiting. This was perfect. The contact was coming to pick her up.

Cortes took out his walkie-talkie; he knew that he could no longer cover this situation on his own.

'This is Cortes. I need backup.'

The customs inspector gave his location, requesting an unmarked car with two plain clothes officers.

Deep on the ocean floor, Mia and her grandfather were not having much luck. They had been searching for the watch for more than ten minutes and had found precisely nothing.

Up on the boat it had seemed obvious where the watch must have fallen. But here on the seabed there was no real way of knowing. No way to orientate, no chance to get a fix on a precise location.

Mia's mask was still leaking. It was almost half full of seawater.

She knew she should clear it, but she couldn't quite remember the correct procedure for doing so. Her grandfather was still finning across the seabed, plunging his hands down into the sea grass in the hope of finding the elusive watch.

Twenty metres or so above her position—on the surface—the teenage girl could see the outline of the tourist craft on which her family were now waiting.

She knew her parents would be getting anxious.

Mia checked her pressure gauge; she had used up a massive percentage of her air.

She continued the fruitless search for the Rolex for a while then she became aware that something had changed; all those big fish that had been swimming happily around had suddenly and mysteriously disappeared. Mia scanned the surrounding area, wondering where on earth all those groupers and tuna had gone.

Something must have caused them to take flight.

But what?

Then she looked up again and she knew exactly what had scared those fish away.

130

The contact turned up at the pickup point. Cortes recognized him immediately—he was Kenny Saula, a known drug distributor and the leader of one of Seattle's many biker gangs.

The stakes had just been raised. Cortes had the uneasy feeling that he might be stumbling into something that was going to get violent.

The biker made his move, approaching the girl and exchanging a few words with her.

Moments later he took the girl by the arm and steered her firmly towards a nearby car park. He slammed some coins into the ticket machine and then took the girl across the parking bays to a dirty looking Chevrolet van which was lurking in a corner.

Cortes waited until the van was on the move, then he saw the unmarked surveillance car waiting for him in a loading area.

Cortes took his seat in the car and the customs team began to follow the Chevrolet, keeping a careful distance as the van weaved through the traffic, heading for the outskirts of the city.

131

Takumi was being blown back down the roof, and the frozen layer of condensation which covered it meant he had no hope of any grip.

He gave up the fight, falling gratefully into the dark with all the suddenness of a light being turned off.

Takumi's unconscious body slid in a graceful line right down the roof, glissading on the wafer thin layer of ice and blown by the ever powerful windblast.

Just as Riku's body had done earlier, it knocked hard into the broken debris of pantograph number seven which was still crashing up and down.

The impact caused the final bolt to fail.

The twisted metal of the pantograph spun up into the air into the two hundred and fifty kilometre an hour slipstream of the train.

132

INTERIOR CHEVROLET VAN, SEATTLE, USA

Mariana was sitting in the passenger seat of the stinking old Chevrolet van. She was exhausted and eaten up with fear but at least she knew that a call had been made to Rio— her sister was safe for the moment, so far as she knew.

Nevertheless she was filled with dread at what the rest of the day would bring. A drug would be given to her to re-start her digestive system. The capsules inside her would have to be expelled from her body and cleaned. The whole process was enough to make her feel thoroughly ill.

Then Mariana felt her stomach twitch. The driver looked at her sharply.

'What's up?' he snapped.

Mariana couldn't reply. Something had changed—it felt as if a cupful of red hot chillies had been suddenly thrown inside her belly.

The capsules of cocaine. Had one burst? Tears of terror pricked her eyes as she felt dozens of needle sharp stabs inside her.

'Stop the car,' she told Kenny. 'I'm going to be sick.'

At first Mia could see about twenty of the sharks, sleek, muscular creatures with an off-white belly and dark black edge to the tail. Each was about three metres long, roughly the length of a saloon car.

Her heart tripped a beat.

She loved sea creatures. But this was a bit too close for comfort.

The sharks were definitely interested in the strange figures standing on the seabed. In fact they were now circling directly above the old man and his granddaughter, blocking their route back up to the boat.

Mia knew in that instant that they were in a seriously screwed-up situation; a lifetime watching documentaries meant she recognized the creatures as Grey Reef sharks, one of the most aggressive and troublesome of all shark species—and regarded by many experts as more deadly than the Great White.

Mia's steady breathing rate collapsed into a ragged series of sharp draws on the regulator as panic set in. Breathe. Breathe. Not so fast. Conserve the air.

Breathe. Breathe. Pant. Pant. One of the sharks swam closer, cruising just a metre or so above the seabed and checking her out at little more than one arm's length.

Seconds later, as she watched through her still faulty goggles, she saw the entire space of water above her fill with at least a *hundred* more of the creatures.

Her grandfather had seen them now. He turned to her and she saw nothing but pure panic in his eyes.

134

As the bullet train sped onwards Saki was still waiting for the guard to leave the door.

It had been a long wait but finally she was rewarded; he slunk off to the lavatory cubicle, leaving the door to the restaurant car momentarily unguarded.

Saki waited until the guard was well out of sight. Then she walked as nonchalantly as she could down the carriage. She ducked underneath the tape that was sealing the corridor off and slipped through the electric door into the restaurant car.

No one was around. Some of the tables still had half eaten meals on them where guests had been hurriedly escorted away before the fumigation.

She looked for signs that Brad had been there—chewed up napkins or his droppings along one of the walls. Nothing. Not a single clue to keep the hope alive.

She knew she wouldn't have long. The guard would be back as soon as he finished in the toilet.

'Brad?' she whispered. 'You there?'

She moved further down the carriage, towards the sealed off area.

135

ON BOARD RESCUE HELICOPTER, HIDA MOUNTAIN RANGE, JAPAN

The pilot saw the broken pantograph fly up towards him but there was nowhere near enough time to react.

The twelve and a half kilo chunk of metal drove itself through the lightweight plexiglass bubble dome of the helicopter cockpit and lodged itself against the rudder controls whilst at the same time shredding the pilot's boot, breaking four of his toes, his heel, and fracturing his ankle.

His scream was so loud through the headphones that the co-pilot thought his ear drums had burst.

On board alarms began to shrill as sensors flashed.

A split second later, a secondary fragment of the metal conductor flew into the tail rotor of the EC135, causing a hairline fracture in a blade.

'Free the controls! Quickly!' the pilot screamed. His co-pilot leaned forward and tried to pull the metal strut away.

The heli lurched towards the train, one of the skids buckling as it hit the roof.

The pilot looked up. Ahead of them was a tunnel, the sheer face of a cliff above it.

136

Customs inspector Cortes saw the Chevrolet van pull onto the verge. The girl was vomiting out of the door. 'The girl's being sick. I think she's got a capsule gone off inside her.'

'Standing by.' A second customs car had joined the tail. Cortes had to make a snap decision. He knew that the girl could easily die if she was not transferred immediately to hospital.

'We have to take him out,' Cortes ordered. 'Go!'

Cortes's vehicle raced up the verge and swerved in front of the Chevrolet. Saula saw the lights coming, knew it was a bust. The second vehicle roared in behind him, ramming him from the rear as three of Cortes's men leapt from the car with weapons drawn. Mariana was thrown to the ground.

'Customs officers!' Cortes yelled.

Saula leapt from the van, tried to make a run for it across the wasteground. But Cortes and his men were too fast for him and he was quickly tackled to the floor.

Cortes turned to the girl, helped her to sit up. She was struggling to breathe, panting as if she'd just fought a pack of lions, covered with dust and dirt.

'Help me get her in the car. There's no time to wait for an ambulance.'

Cortes and two of his men bundled Mariana into the back of the car.

137

Ten thousand four hundred kilometres to the south-west, in the economic powerhouse that is Hong Kong, a financial journalist by the name of Simon Chan was laughing out loud.

Chan was an oil specialist, based at the Asian Oil Exchange building in Hong Kong and a colleague had just sent him the 'Rabid Rat' clip for a laugh.

Chan had watched it with his morning coffee, appreciating it all the more because he knew Otto Krips personally and had often interviewed him.

Chan decided it would make a good diary piece for his daily blog but it needed a quote from one of Krips's associates.

Then he thought of Vincent Bascombe, Otto's boss— and the perfect source for the type of tongue-in-cheek humorous quote he had in mind.

Chan stroked his laptop into life and summoned up his contacts file.

A video call on Skype was quickly under way.

138

SHINKANSEN BULLET TRAIN, EN-ROUTE NAGANO, JAPAN

Saki saw the kitchen zone ahead, realized that the workers had done a thorough job of sealing it—there was heavy duty plastic sheeting from ceiling to floor, all stuck down with the toughest type of duct tape. There wasn't a single chink in the defence; the fumigation team hadn't wanted to take the slightest risk that the gas could leak out.

'Brad?' she whispered again.

She reached out and picked up a steak knife which had been left on a table. She would have to cut her way through the barrier.

It was tough. Surprisingly tough. Making some effort, she sliced through it, creating a slit about a metre long, and poked her head inside.

'Brad? Are you still alive?'

Then she gasped as the poison entered her lungs.

A single breath was enough to demonstrate to Saki quite what a mistake she had made.

The burning sensation was instantaneous; an unbearable acid pain as the moist membranes of her throat, nose, and eyes were attacked by the gas.

Saki uttered a strangled scream of shock, then she ran from the carriage, heading for the toilet cubicle.

She tried the handle. The door was locked.

Saki sprinted for the far end of the carriage, found a vacant toilet. Half blind, she ripped open the door and rushed inside, splashing cool handfuls against her face . . .

More water. More water.

139
PARADA DE LUCAS, RIO DE JANEIRO, BRAZIL

Leonardo's son Casio was released from casualty as soon as his treatment finished. His broken left arm had been re-set and immobilized in a plaster cast which stretched from his hand to his elbow.

One of his father's guards came to pick him up, telling him about the fiasco at the rubbish dump and taking him back to the drug lord's base.

His father was out on business. Word was that he had a problem with a drug shipment into the US.

Casio was feeling sore. The cheap rum he'd drunk earlier had given him a savage headache and he was filled with shame for how things had worked out after the car crash.

He should have killed that kid, Remo, when he had the chance. That pig-boy had humiliated him in front of his father, damaging the Hummer, caused him to be injured and showing him nothing but disrespect.

One of his father's favourite sayings was running through Casio's head:

'You're not a man until you've killed a man.'

Casio took a loaded handgun from his father's safe and walked out into the dark night of the *favela*.

The cliff face was right before the heli. The bullet train vanished with a rush into a tunnel as the pilots frantically tried to manoeuvre themselves out of a fatal impact.

'Climb! Climb!' the pilot commanded.

The heli was getting faster and faster. The airspeed control systems had been damaged and the power units were running out of control. Smoke was spewing out of the front panel.

The co-pilot yanked with all his strength on the collective and the EC135 laboured heavily as the rotors punched enough air to—just—scrape them over the top of the cliff.

The lake was before them, the silver tracks of the railway line snaking around it.

The Shinkansen still hadn't come out of the tunnel.

'Pull back your foot!' The co-pilot tried again to free the metal obstruction. No success.

At that moment the hairline fracture of the tail rotor suddenly widened under the continuous pressure of the spinning blade.

The tail rotor splintered and broke.

'Avoid the tracks! Avoid the tracks!'

The call was too late. The EC135 crashed onto the railway tracks on the lake edge, the rotor and tail rotor splintering as the aircraft tipped onto its side in a violent cartwheel and juddered to a standstill in a haze of white smoke.

141

Cortes's assistant was at the wheel of the unmarked customs vehicle as it raced down the street towards the Mayfield Hospital. Cortes was in the back, trying to keep the girl from blacking out.

'Don't go to sleep,' he repeated, 'you have to stay awake no matter how bad you feel.'

Mariana stared at him with feverish eyes, then she vomited into the passenger footwell of the car.

'That's good,' Cortes encouraged her, 'be sick. That'll get the drugs out of you.'

The moment they arrived at casualty Cortes picked the girl up in his arms and ran for the entrance. There was no time to waste waiting for a hospital porter to arrive.

As soon as he had explained the case, Mariana was placed on a trolley bed. She was immediately wheeled down the corridor towards a waiting team of ER medics.

As he waited outside the operating theatre, Cortes saw three security guards rush past at high speed. They had stun guns and coshes drawn.

What next? It's all happening today, Cortes thought, there really isn't a dull moment in this city.

142

NIHUE ISLAND, HAWAII, PACIFIC OCEAN

If she had been watching the scene on a television documentary, Mia would have been awestruck.

There was a primeval sense of majesty about this huge gathering of predators, a choreographed synchronicity in the way they moved, a collective sense of *purpose* which was at the same time sinister and sublime.

But the sixteen-year-old girl was not watching this incredible wildlife on her forty-two inch plasma screen back in Sausalito, California. She was watching it from the distinctly less desirable viewpoint of the seabed, twenty metres beneath the boat where her family were waiting.

Mia checked her gauge.

She had about five minutes of air left, assuming she could get her breathing under control.

Breathe. Breathe. Slower. Slower. Save the air.

Vincent pointed behind her, towards the small cave which was set into the seabed. She understood immediately, swimming towards it and nestling herself into the rocky crevasse.

She gestured for Vincent to squeeze in beside her and he finned over and managed to wedge himself into the crevice.

Mia checked her gauge again. Four minutes of air.

And still the sharks were getting closer.

143

Mariana was wheeled, barely conscious, into the medical theatre and placed on her side on the operating table.

An X-ray was taken. The ER team could see the ghostly outline of the dozens of drug capsules inside her stomach.

'She's one of the lucky ones,' the surgeon told Cortes, 'the capsules haven't moved further down into her system. And they're small enough to be suctioned out. We can do this the easy way.'

A staff nurse injected her with a sedative dose of Midazolam and the drug mule's world went pleasingly dark from that point as all her pain receded.

As soon as she was tranquillized, a lubricated rubber tube was gently passed down her oesophagus and into her stomach.

A suction device was attached to the tube and the contents of Mariana's stomach were gently sucked out.

Warm saline solution was then pumped into her, washing the stomach completely clean, until the contents ran clear.

'She'll have a heck of a headache when she wakes up,' the surgeon told Cortes, 'but she's going to be fine. We caught it just in time.'

144

The bullet train hit the wreckage of the EC135 Eurocopter at just over two hundred and fifty kilometres an hour. The driver didn't even have time to activate the braking system it happened so fast.

When a train that size is travelling at 83.333 metres per second, there is not much margin for action when an obstacle suddenly appears just a couple of hundred metres ahead.

The nose of the bullet train punched into the helicopter in a tortured shriek of fragmented metal and a roar of combusted aviation fuel as the heli tank exploded.

The impact was enough to lift the front end of the bullet train bodily off the tracks. For slightly less than a second the leading edge of the train was airborne by about thirty or forty centimetres.

Then it smashed back down to earth and from that point on the train was derailed.

145

INTERNATIONAL ASIAN OIL EXCHANGE, HONG KONG, CHINA

Simon Chan got through to Vincent Bascombe's laptop with a Skype video call but the person pictured on the other end of the line was certainly not the oil man.

The fuzzy picture on Chan's screen appeared to be a stressed-out eight-year-old boy. Sitting in what looked like the cabin of a boat.

'Who is this?' the boy asked. He was struggling to make himself heard above a cacophony of shouts and yells in the background.

'Can I speak to Vincent Bascombe please?'

'You can't,' the kid gushed, 'he's being . . . surrounded, attacked by sharks. We used the snorkelling masks, looked over the side. We think . . . we don't know what's happening. The captain says they're in serious danger. My sister's down there too!'

The kid sounded absolutely beside himself.

'*He's being attacked by sharks?*' Chan was astounded by this development. 'What do you mean by that exactly?'

146

Remo was still trudging through the night, searching for Leonardo's compound. He was weary to his young bones, striding with stubborn determination up and down the winding stairways of the slum.

Where was that gate? The one with the dragon graffiti. So far he had seen no sign of it.

He had to find that girl. Find a way to rescue her.

His feet were aching, and he had blisters where his old sneakers had worn through and split.

Then he spotted someone he knew. The last person he wanted to see.

Casio. Leonardo's son. Prowling those same streets.

Remo hid in the shadows, wondering what the thug was doing. He was searching for someone, that much was clear.

Remo knew then that his troubles were far from over.

147
MAYFIELD HOSPITAL, SEATTLE, USA

The armed response team arrived at the Mayfield Hospital just a short time after the emergency call. They got a fast verbal briefing from the in-house security guys and were told that Nelson had a man hostage.

'We know this guy's got a taser,' the police chief told his men. 'We have to assume he has a gun as well.'

The policemen ran up to the third floor of a building opposite the hospital where they identified a room which had a perfect line of sight right into the room where Nelson and the guard were ensconsed.

The police chief quickly focused his binoculars on the scene. 'He's surfing the net,' the police chief said. 'What the heck's he playing at?'

In his experience, crazed gunmen didn't take security guards hostage so they could then sit around at a computer looking at the internet.

'No idea, chief. But he looks kinda crazy.'

148

Customs Inspector Cortes was sitting by Mariana's hospital bed as her eyes flickered, opened a little.

'What have they done to me?' Her voice was hoarse, and so quiet he had to bend down close to hear her.

'You've had your stomach pumped out,' Cortes told her, 'and the capsules of drugs removed.'

'I feel sick. Help me.' Cortes and a nurse helped the Brazilian girl to sit up as she retched into a bowl.

She sipped some water, then sat up, suddenly more alert as she looked at Cortes.

'My sister,' she told him, 'they're going to kill her when they find out I've lost the drugs.'

'There's nothing I can do about that,' Cortes told her with regret. 'I've already saved *your* life today. I can't do the same for your sister I'm afraid.'

She clutched his hand in a desperate gesture.

'No! You must help me. *Please? You must be able to do something.*'

149

HIDA MOUNTAIN RANGE, JAPAN

Shingle from the crushed stone ballast spewed with near bullet-like velocity as the steel wheels of the engine chewed up the concrete sleepers.

The helicopter crew were torn limb from limb by the incredible force of the impact, their flesh stripped from their bones by hydrostatic force.

The train driver was decapitated by the snapped off carbon fibre rotor blade of the EC135. It punched through the toughened glass window of the bullet train as easily as a warm knife passes through melted butter.

In the split second that followed, burning aviation fuel ignited. The fractured remains of the driver's cab were instantly consumed by fire.

150

Cortes ran the options through his mind as Mariana pleaded with him to help her save her sister.

He was within his rights to refuse. But he was a family man and, deep down, he felt sorry for this girl. He wanted to help her if he possibly could.

Then he remembered the mobile he had just taken from Mariana's captor.

'Did the guy who picked you up make a call to Rio?' he asked.

Mariana thought hard: 'Yes. I think he did.'

Cortes opened up the phone, selected last number redial and cracked a big smile.

'Looks like we got a lead,' he said. 'What was the name of the guy that forced you to take the drugs?'

'Leonardo.'

Cortes thought fast. 'I'm going to call my contact in the Rio drug squad,' he told her. 'We might be able to do something for your sister after all.'

151

The more Simon Chan listened to Danny Bascombe's story the more amazed he became.

Sharks? Running out of air? Was this a hoax?

It certainly didn't seem like one. The kid was genuinely distraught.

'They're sending some more oxygen down,' the kid yelled into the laptop. 'I gotta go!'

'No, stay on the line!' the journalist begged him. 'I might be able to help you.'

Simon Chan was no longer thinking about his boring diary piece. This was a much hotter story. There is nothing like a breaking news item to get a journalist's juices going.

Vincent Bascombe's life in danger? Surrounded by killer sharks?

Simon Chan decided to post an immediate newsflash direct onto Reuters. This was a story that deserved to go global.

152

Mariana's sister Ester had fallen into a restless sleep on the soiled old mattress in her cell.

Then voices in the courtyard woke her up.

A mobile phone rang. She heard her name mentioned.

What was happening? Why were they talking about her? And what had they done to Remo?

She clasped the little golden cross in her hand. The one that Remo had passed to her through the vent.

'Please, God, save me. Save me, please.'

She had heard her mother pray often enough. Had sometimes joined her out of a sense of duty. But this time was for real. The eight-year-old girl was in mortal terror for her life.

153

SHINKANSEN BULLET TRAIN, EN-ROUTE NAGANO, JAPAN

Saki was dousing her face in the toilet of carriage number four, trying to wash the stinging pain of the gas out of her eyes, when the train came off the tracks.

The first thing she felt was a sickening sensation of weightlessness; as if she was in one of those Nasa zero gravity flight simulators. That was the carriage taking off as it hit the one in front. Then there was a ripping sound of torn metal—as if some giant can opener was slicing through the skin of the carriage.

Then the world began to turn as the carriage flipped.

Saki was rammed against the toilet floor as the carriage rolled, then back against the ceiling as it went three-sixty.

Her neck was twisted so hard she could feel her spine on the point of breaking. Her scalp was opened up by a huge cut and her collarbone had snapped as she put out her arms to try and cushion herself against the wall of the cubicle.

Customs Inspector Cortes placed the phone handset down. He had been on the line to Juliana Amadeu in Rio.

He was energized by the call. The adrenaline was running.

'OK,' he told Mariana, 'we're going to try and free your sister from these killers.'

Cortes handed Mariana the mobile.

'You're going to speak to Leonardo. He'll pick up when he sees it's from Kenny's number. I've given the same number to my contact in Rio and they're going to scan it to try and trace the call. That way they can determine the location, and send in a team to find your sister before they kill her.'

'OK.' Mariana's eyes were shining with hope.

'It's a risk,' Cortes told her. 'You'll be bluffing them and they may just lose their patience and kill her anyway. You understand that? OK. Now, here's what you have to say.'

155

Meanwhile, on the seabed, Mia and Vincent were down to their last three minutes of air.

Breathe. Breathe. Stretch the air out to the max. Anything rather than swim out into that circulating mass of predators.

Mia was twisting this way and that as she tried to get a fix on the encroaching monsters. Twenty, maybe thirty of the sharks had taken up station on the seabed; they were getting bolder, losing their fear of these odd looking creatures with their bubbles and their palpable smell of fear.

What was happening up on the boat, Mia wondered? Had they leaned over the side? Seen the threat?

Help from above was their only hope.

The water in Mia's mask was almost up to her eyes. She was getting close to a total panic attack. How many minutes did they have left? Check the regulator. Maybe two. If they were lucky.

Here comes another.

156

Leonardo the drug lord was halfway through a game of cards, knocking back some beers with some of his gang buddies, when his mobile buzzed.

He flinched when he saw the American caller ID number on the screen. It was Kenny. Again. But why so soon?

'Hello, my friend. Everything OK with the delivery?'

To his surprise he now heard the voice of Mariana, the drug mule.

'Something's gone wrong,' she told him. 'Things have got screwed up.'

Leonardo closed his eyes for a beat. Her words had caused his heart to race briefly out of control. His financial backers would go absolutely ape if the drugs were somehow lost.

And it could be his head on the chopping block.

'Where's Kenny?'

'He's dead.'

157

INTERNATIONAL ASIAN OIL EXCHANGE, HONG KONG, CHINA

The newsflash came up on the Reuters international website. Chan's report stated that renowned oil veteran Vincent Bascombe had 'failed to return from a dive' after a reported 'shark attack' whilst on holiday.

Oil prices rise and fall for a thousand and one reasons and they do so at lightning speed. Rumours of a hurricane in the Caribbean can send the price of a barrel of crude oil up more than a dollar if traders fear Venezuela's prolific operation will be hit. A pirate attack on an oil tanker in the Bight of Benin off the west coast of Africa can have a similar effect.

And that was why the news that Vincent Bascombe, the head of one of America's biggest independent oil companies, had been 'attacked by sharks', increased the value of oil—within minutes—by a couple of cents.

It wasn't much of a gain. But it pushed the price of a barrel of crude oil above ninety dollars—a trigger point for movement for certain players in the oil game.

158

The engine and passenger carriage number one slid at high speed—still coupled in a V-shaped formation—across the valley floor as flames raged through them.

Forty-seven passengers were killed in that carriage.

Carriage number two went airborne, sliding across rough terrain on its roof at more than two hundred kilometres an hour then slamming into a boulder field on the forest edge.

Sixty-five passengers were killed in that carriage.

Carriage number three rolled twice in a mist of torn up earth and shattered glass. The forty-three tonne wheel and axle assembly was ripped from the chassis of the train by the blow as it hit the ground, the massive metal missile twisting through the air before it fell into the forest where it demolished twenty or more substantial trees.

159

As soon as Mariana's call had got through to the Rio-based mobile, Juliana Amadeu ran the mobile number into the database at the narcotics agency. Sitting alongside her were two radio and telephone experts from the agency.

Their job would be to locate the whereabouts of the mobile, using the nearest cellphone transmitters to triangulate the position and pin it down as far as they could.

Then the hit squad would go in.

She had plenty of firepower at her command. Seven vehicle-based fast-response units were spread around the city. A police Sikorsky helicopter was sitting on the helipad at that very moment with rotors turning and three highly trained armed response officers on board.

Moments later the database came back with a positive check on the mobile.

'OK, we're doing the trace now.'

160

At that moment, some five thousand kilometres to the north-west, an oil tanker received a radio call.

The vessel was the *Eckmann Conveyor 2* and she was sitting stationary at anchor with a full load of crude oil just a short distance from the coast of Venezuela.

She had been there for more than two months, staffed with a skeleton crew, waiting for the price of crude oil to go up before setting sail for her home port of Rio.

These tactics are common when oil prices are low.

Now, as the price of a barrel of oil clicked up that final magical tenth of a cent to ninety dollars a barrel, the consortium radioed a command through to Captain Stevamedes, the Greek merchant marine officer in charge of the vessel.

The cargo had been sold, the message confirmed, and the captain was to set sail for Rio as soon as he could.

161

Casio arrived at the pig yard where Remo had his shack. The thug had been breaking and entering for years and the lock on the doorway was no match for someone with his experience.

He forced it with a screwdriver and quietly entered the yard. The pigs were asleep and he crossed quickly to the little shack in the corner and pulled back the corrugated iron sheet that served as a door.

He rushed the room, pistol at the ready, but found it was empty.

The pig-boy wasn't back yet. Probably still rooting around in those disgusting piles of rubbish, searching for scraps.

Casio replaced the corrugated iron sheet behind him in the doorway and crouched in the darkest corner of the room.

The kid had to sleep sometime. And the moment he appeared in that doorway he was going to get it. A first notch on Casio's gun handle. Something to make his father proud.

Casio waited in the pitch black, his finger on the trigger, all senses alert.

162

HIDA MOUNTAIN RANGE, JAPAN

Most of the passengers were thrown out of the broken windows by the twisting force of the rolling carriage, only to be crushed in their dozens beneath it before the kinetic energy of the collision was dissipated.

Sam and Cody—the two American travellers who had filmed the rat incident—were amongst those victims.

Carriage number four was simply crushed, the seventy metre long metal tube concertinaed by the impacting forces of the carriages behind it into a cube some eight metres long.

Everyone in that carriage died, including Otto Krips—the German who had been bitten by the rat—and his wife.

The remaining four carriages suffered a different fate.

They went straight into the mountain lake.

And sank immediately out of sight.

163

Twenty metres beneath the seas off the island of Nihue in Hawaii, Vincent Bascombe and his granddaughter Mia were sucking urgently on their regulators as their air rapidly ran out.

The moment was coming up fast. The moment when they would have to quit the sanctuary of the cave.

Two huge sharks swam within striking distance of the cave. Victor lunged out courageously at both attackers, managing to hit one a sharp blow on the snout and jabbing the other in the eye.

But both divers knew such resistance was futile—there were just too many of the sharks showing an interest and all it would take would be the scent of one drop of blood . . .

Then they saw the object being lowered down from above.

An air tank! They must have seen the sharks from the boat!
A chance of salvation. Or at least a stay of execution.

164

As the mighty engines of the *Eckmann Conveyor 2* built up revs ready to begin the journey to South America, one particular crew member put down his cleaning materials and ran for the ship's communication room.

His name was Carlito, a native of Rio—the *Eckmann Conveyor*'s home port. Carlito had had a chaotic life; alcoholism and gambling had caused him to split from his wife and his son Remo. For two guilt-filled years he had roamed the world on this oil tanker, making no contact with them. But recently he had changed; he had stopped drinking, even reading the Bible from time to time.

Now he was going home to Rio. And he was determined to make amends. He wanted to hold his wife in his arms once again, watch his son grow into a man.

'Do me a favour,' Carlito asked the radio operator, 'can I send a quick email?'

'OK,' the man pushed the keyboard towards Carlito, 'go ahead. But make it quick, amigo.'

'Thanks. I'll buy you a beer when we get to Rio.'

165

HIDA MOUNTAIN RANGE, JAPAN

Professor Yamada was just seventy metres from the impact.

He ducked for cover; the air filled with spinning chunks of debris. Splinters of shattered trees showered the zone.

The noise was simply horrific—the initial explosion followed immediately by the sickening sound of chewed up metal, devastated trees, and the eerie whine of axles and drive gear as they powered the bullet train at more than two hundred kilometres an hour into a million pieces of so much scrap.

For a few seconds all was sound and fury.

Then came a world filled with nothing but the hiss of a few spinning steel wheels and the roar of numerous fuel-derived fires.

166

Mariana had to concentrate hard to get the story right. But she knew her sister's life could depend on it as she kept Leonardo on the line in Rio.

'Kenny met me at a mall,' she told him. 'We were driving away . . . back to his place. Then some men came alongside in a car and tried to stop us. They shot him.'

Leonardo swore heavily.

'He fired back,' Mariana continued, 'the men in the car disappeared, Kenny managed to keep driving . . . got us back to his flat. But then . . . then he died.'

'You're in his flat now?'

'Yes.'

'Look. The most important thing is the consignment,' Leonardo told her. 'If you end up losing those drugs, your sister is going to suffer and she is going to die. Do you understand me?'

'I guess so. I'm just so scared about everything. I don't know what to do. Tell me again what I have to do.'

167

As the *Eckmann Conveyor 2* oil tanker reached full revs, powering through the ocean with its precious load of crude, Carlito the cleaner clicked on to his email account and composed the message to a certain missionary he knew in the *favela* back home.

He knew the man would track down Remo and give him the message:

'My dear son. I have been out of your lives for too long. Please tell your mother I am coming home and that everything will be different this time. My ship just got the orders to sail for Rio. I'll be home in two weeks. I hope you can forgive me for all this time away. Papa.'

He hit the return tab and the message was instantly flying through the ether on its way to his son.

Moments later he was busily back at work, cleaning out the toilet cubicles, whistling a happy tune. Soon he would be with his family.

168

Vincent knew he had no choice. He had to swim out of the cave to get to the oxygen tank.

He launched himself out of the refuge, feeling his own air supply falter and die as he did so.

Suddenly, the snout of a shark struck a glancing blow on Vincent's thigh. The blow was a forceful one; it was like being side-swiped with a fast moving block of concrete. The old man could tell he had come within an ace of getting his thigh bone smashed.

The predator moved away with a swift kick of its tail.

With trembling hands, Vincent managed to snap his air line onto the new bottle, twisted open the valve and thrust the regulator into his mouth.

He swam back to Mia so he could share the regulator with her.

Then he checked the gauge.

The bottle lowered down would buy them another four minutes at most.

169

PARADA DE LUCAS, RIO DE JANEIRO, BRAZIL

Ester heard the rasp of the rusty bolts on the door.

The sound she had come to fear above all others.

A flashlight dazzled her.

The same men that had kidnapped her entered the cell.

'Your time has come,' one of the men told her. 'Leonardo has asked us to take you on a little trip.'

She shrank back against the wall. But their strong hands jerked her upright in a second. She struggled for a moment but was stilled by a brutal string of swear words from her captors.

They dragged the small girl out into the courtyard of the compound where a vehicle was waiting.

Where was the boy—Remo? He had promised to help her but he was nowhere to be seen.

170

Roger Stansfield was one of the lucky ones.

He was thrown clear of the carriage as it sank into the lake, losing consciousness for a brief moment before reviving abruptly as the super chilled water embraced his skin.

If the academic hadn't been such a strong swimmer, he might have drowned there and then. A certain quantity of water had entered his lungs and as he trod water he coughed violently, gagging until he managed to control his breathing and recover his composure.

Nearer to the shore, the lake surface was actually on *fire*—spilt aviation fuel from the helicopter was burning furiously. Stansfield swam to the nearest place he could grab hold of—the top of a carriage which had landed sticking proud of the water.

A dozen or more traumatized survivors were swimming towards the same spot.

Then Stansfield remembered the girl. The last thing he remembered before the crash was seeing Saki rush to the toilet—the 'click' of the door.

She was down there. Trapped inside.

BUREAU OF NARCOTICS INVESTIGATION, RIO DE JANEIRO, BRAZIL

'How are we doing with the location fix on the mobile?' Juliana asked.

'One more minute,' the expert told her.

'Keep talking,' Juliana prayed, thinking about the brave girl in Seattle who was even now stringing out the conversation with Leonardo. 'Just don't hang up.'

'OK. We got them nailed.' The comms man wrote some co-ordinates down on a pad. He showed Juliana the position on the map of the *Parada de Lucas* slum.

'They're in the high part of the *favela*. Within fifty metres of the old water tower.'

'Nice work.'

Juliana Amadeu crossed to a steel cabinet and swung her bullet-proof vest out of its holder.

Remo kept moving, street after street, praying that he would stumble across the compound and keeping a look out for Casio.

The slum was so huge. The compound could be anywhere.

Then something very unexpected happened: he was passing one of the small makeshift chapels of the *favela* when a voice hissed out: 'Hey, Remo!'

It was a nightwatchman—a kindly soul that occasionally bought swill from the pig-boy.

'I just got a call on my mobile. A message arrived for you at the mission. Email. They're printing it out for you.'

Remo's spirit soared. A rare and almost forgotten sensation coursed through him; the warm glow of something called *hope*.

An email for him could only be from one person. *His father.*

Remo thanked the nightwatchman and ran full tilt towards the mission complex far across the other side of the *favela*. When he reached it he looked across the road where his attention was grabbed by something familiar:

A gate with graffiti. A painting of a dragon.

173

Nelson checked the visitors register on his blog site: *eight hundred and fifty thousand* people were looking at the grab frames of the bullet train kids.

'We gotta hit a million!' he told Paco on the Skype connection.

Nelson's mind was foaming with the adrenaline of it all. He had never known a thrill so intense. This was the sweet spot of his trainspotting career, a once in a lifetime convergence where the world stood up and finally recognized Nelson F. Muster for the person he was—a person of global significance. Then he heard a cry from the casualty room.

'Armed police! Come out with your hands in the air.'

'Screw you!' he shouted back.

Jeez, the computer was getting slow.

Then Nelson's world came skidding to a stop. The train-spotter site had ground to a halt.

'Hey! What's *happening*?' Nelson slammed his fist against the desk in a rage.

174

HIDA MOUNTAIN RANGE, JAPAN

Stansfield trod water for a few seconds as he looked down into the depths. He could see the outline of the carriage, lying on its side at a depth of about ten metres.

Stansfield took a huge breath, then he duck-dived, pulling down with a powerful breast-stroke as he struck out for the sunken carriage.

He reached the carriage, touched the sharp edge of shattered glass on the window lip.

Then he pulled himself inside, his body already screaming for air.

Stansfield took a look around; there was a small air bubble trapped in the ceiling there and he took the opportunity to snatch a few breaths.

The toilet door was right in front of him.

Yes! A muffled noise. Banging. The sound of a girl screaming!

She was still alive.

175

Remo banged on the mission door, managed to wake one of the priests and he was handed the precious message from his father.

He read it with trembling hands. It was true! He was coming home!

He would be bringing a pay packet with him that would change their lives in so many ways.

Then Remo remembered the kidnapped girl. He begged the priest to let him use a telephone but the man was reluctant to let this dirty boy loose in the mission office and he refused.

Remo was firmly escorted back onto the street where he hid in the shadows, watching the compound.

Minutes later the door opened and he caught a glimpse of the girl being loaded into the back of a truck by two of Leonardo's henchmen.

The pickup set off into the deepest part of the slum.

Remo decided to try and follow it.

He saw a moped in the mission yard. He climbed onto it and kicked it into life.

176

Juliana Amadeu clipped the Kevlar protection vest over her shirt and shrugged her jacket over the top. She plugged her mobile into a headset and placed it carefully in position. The unit would give her a live feed from the control room, and also enable her to speak to Cortes in Seattle to update him on the raid.

'I'm going to get a pick up from the heli,' she told her colleagues.

Seconds later, her weapon safely tucked into a shoulder harness, she was running down the corridor.

Out on the heli pad the police Sikorsky helicopter was waiting.

Juliana took her seat next to her colleagues and the heli spun up into the Rio night, heading for the Parada de Lucas.

177

SHINKANSEN BULLET TRAIN, HIDA MOUNTAIN LAKE, JAPAN

In the toilet cubicle, the water was rising. It was up to Saki's chest, freezing and all embracing. The cubicle was two-thirds full and she had no idea how much time she had left before her face would be submerged. She shifted her position so that her mouth was higher—anything to give her a few more breaths.

She kicked again at the door—but the water acted as a drag and it was no more than a token blow against the solid plastic moulding.

Then came a blinding moment of hope.

The door handle was turning! Someone was out there!

Saki kicked out harder, beat against the ceiling with her hands. She had to make *noise*, let a possible rescuer know that she was in here—and alive!

The water was curling up higher—now it was up to her neck.

178

Simon Chan still had the young kid on the Skype call to the boat. The screams and cries in the background were louder and more harrowing by the moment.

'Is there anything I can do to help?' the journalist asked him. 'Make an emergency call or something?'

'The captain says we need a shark cage to bring them both up,' the boy sobbed. 'But we haven't got one.'

The journo racked his brain; he was a diver himself and he wanted to play his part if he could. Then he spotted something on the Skype picture.

The metal frame of a double decker bunk bed in the rear of the cabin. It looked like a heavy piece of furniture, constructed from steel.

'You see the bunk bed behind you?' Chan said. The kid looked round uncertainly. 'It's like a cage, isn't it? Tell the captain to send it down on a line. Your sister and your grandpa might be able to get inside it and they can bring them up.'

179

Leonardo's thugs raced up the final stretch of *favela* track and screamed to a halt on a dirty patch of wasteland which was dotted with burned out wrecks.

Seconds later, Remo arrived on the moped, hot on their trail.

The street kid parked up, melted into the shadows. Watching all the while. Thanking God they hadn't seen him.

There was a drinking shack nearby. A notorious place which had long been associated with Leonardo and his team.

Remo saw the men look around cautiously. Then they pulled the young girl from the back of the pickup and bundled her into the drinking den.

Remo moved stealthily to the side of the shack.

He wished he had a mobile phone, a way to alert the drug cop to what was going on.

Should he run to find help? The cop station was miles away.

180

Stansfield could hear the muffled impacts coming from within the toilet cubicle. He was on the limit of his air endurance and fighting a growing sense of panic which threatened to overwhelm him.

He pressed his weight against the door. It didn't give at all. Then he tried again, feeling the door move as he got his shoulder lower.

The door was open! He could see the girl.

He burst up into the air cavity.

'I'm taking you out,' he managed to gasp. 'You'll have to swim through the carriage with me.'

She didn't respond but merely whimpered with fear.

'Hold my hand.'

He felt her fingers close round his with extraordinary power.

Stansfield and the girl took a final huge breath and left the cubicle for the carriage corridor.

181

HIDA MOUNTAIN RANGE, JAPAN

Yamada crawled across the grass and reached the closest of the carriages. It was flat on its side, with part of the roof peeled back and open. Inside he could see mangled tables and chairs, along with broken crockery and other debris.

He realized it must have been a restaurant car. He pulled himself up onto the edge of the carriage but could see no survivors inside. The car must have been empty, he decided, when the accident happened—or perhaps everyone had been thrown out.

Then Yamada heard something strange.

Scratching—somewhere in the wreckage.

Was there someone alive after all?

'Hello?' he called. 'Is there someone there? Are you trapped?'

No reply. But then the scratching started again.

182

Mariana's little sister Ester was manhandled into the room.

Bright light dazzled. Calloused hands grabbed at her ankles and wrists. A dozen men were leering at her.

The room stank of cheap beer and acrid body odour.

The men stared at her with emotionless, alcohol-hazed eyes.

'Put her over there,' one of the men ordered.

Ester was thrown violently onto a pile of old carpet in the corner of the room. She landed awkwardly, hurting her arm.

Leonardo stared at her as she let out a cry of pain.

'We are talking to your sister,' he told her. 'Her actions will decide if you will live or die.'

183

Roger Stansfield burst up onto the surface of the lake and sucked so much air into his lungs he felt he was going to explode. The girl had gone limp but he still had her by the hand. He twisted onto his back and supported her body as he kicked out for the shallow water of the lake's edge where other survivors were already wading in to help him.

The fire had burned itself out, leaving a shroud of greasy black smoke hanging over the scene.

Together they got the girl onto the grass at the lake shore.

Stansfield placed his lips to the Japanese girl's mouth. He gently blew warm air into her lungs, once, twice, three times, then paused to pump her chest.

The girl seemed drowned, her eyes had rolled back, her lips were blue.

184

As soon as the skids of the Sikorsky touched down on the wasteground, Juliana Amadeu and her team were out of the aircraft and running. They knew this crime-blighted district of old, well enough to know that speed was essential if they wanted to get their man.

In the *Parada de Lucas* there are a thousand pairs of eyes ready to raise the alarm when the police come to call.

Juliana's mind was in overdrive:

Where was the girl? Could they save her?

The fix on the mobile had given them an area to search but it wasn't precise enough to tell them Leonardo's *exact* location.

He was somewhere near the old water tower. But it could still take them time to find him.

Time that the eight-year-old girl didn't have.

185

HIDA MOUNTAIN RANGE, JAPAN

The scratching noise continued, more frantic now.

It sounded exactly as though someone was rasping their nails on a metal surface.

Professor Yamada decided he would investigate. He crawled across the wreckage of the restaurant car and pulled at a huge sheet of crumpled metal which he guessed had once been the floor.

He tugged harder at the metal sheet and it suddenly gave way with a sharp sound of rendering aluminium.

At that moment a rat ran out.

A rat? The professor jumped back, absolutely amazed.

What on earth would a rat be doing in the wreckage of this bullet train?

The creature saw daylight—ran for the door.

186

When she saw the bunk bed frame being lowered down towards the seabed, Mia Bascombe thought she was hallucinating.

Then her grandfather Vincent tuned into the logic of what they had done.

He pulled the metal frame towards them and Mia finally got it.

The steel structure of the bunk bed would offer them shelter if they could jam themselves inside it.

Mia went first. She squirmed into the metal frame with some difficulty, hauling the cylinder of air with her.

Vincent followed on, jamming himself into the improvised cage next to her. The sharks kept their distance, not trusting this shiny contraption.

A moment later, the bed frame began to rise.

And that was when Vincent saw the flash of gold.

The watch. Lying on the bottom. Just a body length away, glistening amongst the sea grass.

187

The slum dwellers scattered in alarm as they saw Juliana and her uniformed team racing up the alleyways.

Keep moving fast. Ignore the pain.

Juliana felt a stitch grip her side. She was struggling to keep up with her fitter colleagues. Don't stop now. Leonardo is there for the taking.

There was the water tower.

They were getting closer. In the zone.

But only a house-to-house search would flush Leonardo out.

'Which way, boss?' Juliana felt a rising sensation of panic. How would they find Leonardo's exact location? There were hundreds of places he could be.

Then she saw a figure she recognized. He was standing next to a shack.

It was Remo—the kid she had saved from the incinerator.

188

The computer screen was still frozen.

The server had crashed. The ride was over.

Nelson looked at the dead screen. He knew then that he would never get his millionth online hit.

The trainspotter suddenly felt more tired and alone than he'd ever felt before. All he wanted in that moment was to slip back home to his monitors, his comfort food, his medication and the ever present attention of his long-suffering mother.

'Come out now!' the megaphone intoned from the corridor. 'Or we are going to storm the room.'

'OK,' he called. 'I'm coming out.'

Nelson flipped the lock on the door and walked unsteadily out into the casualty room where he was astonished to find a dozen or so armed policemen arranged in key positions of cover.

Every single one of them had a weapon trained on him.

189

Saki's glazed eyes gradually cleared as she gagged the water free from her lungs.

Stansfield's last-ditch attempt to revive her had worked.

She began to shiver, clutching on to Roger Stansfield's hand with a vice-like grip as the physical shock of the last five minutes engulfed her.

Then she saw something that made her gasp with surprise and delight.

A rat was walking unsteadily across the meadow.

'Brad?' Saki called to the rat with wonder in her voice.

The rat stopped—looked towards Saki.

He looked as if he had been through a war, with singed fur and a couple of superficial cuts.

But he still knew her voice.

190

Mariana almost cried out with relief when Leonardo told her:

'Your sister is here in the room.'

'Can I talk to her? I want to hear her voice.'

'First we need information. What has happened to the delivery?'

'Let me talk to my sister . . . I want to talk to my sister.'

'Mariana . . . Mariana . . . ' There was no mistaking the deadly intent in his tone, 'we need to know where you are and what you are doing with the merchandise. Your sister is in big trouble here.'

'Don't hurt her, please God don't hurt her.'

Mariana heard her sister scream in the background.

'Too late,' Leonardo snarled. 'I'm going to cut her throat in twenty seconds if you don't give me a guarantee that our merchandise is safe.'

191
MAYFIELD HOSPITAL, SEATTLE, USA

Nelson stared at the officers as the order came:

'Put your hands over your head then lie down face forward on the floor!'

Nelson's right hand twitched as he felt the mobile vibrate against his chest.

He knew it would be Paco calling and he knew that Paco must have some new information about his crashed site. Maybe it was even running again.

'Put your hands in the air!'

The mobile continued to vibrate and as it did so all of Nelson's good intentions of peaceful surrender went flying out of the window. He was just itching to know what Paco had discovered.

He just knew that call would be Paco. Maybe they could still make those million hits.

No question about it. Nelson F. Muster absolutely *had* to take that call. He hurriedly brought down his right arm and reached into the inside pocket of his jacket.

192

Juliana was about to lead her team towards the water tower when Remo suddenly saw her.

'You are going the wrong way!' the pig-boy called out. 'Come with me.'

Juliana had to go on gut instinct. And her instinct was: *I trust this boy.*

Amadeu turned her SWAT team around and they followed Remo back to the small drinking shack where the drama was unfolding.

'In there!' Remo told them.

Juliana Amadeu already had the pin pulled on the stun grenade.

193

Vincent Bascombe had always been an impulsive risk taker. He was a rash and impetuous man who often acted first and thought later.

But this was the day when he took a risk too far as he made a mad dash to try and retrieve that precious watch.

As soon as he had the watch in his hand the first shark struck.

The impact was a bone-shattering blow to the shoulder. A significant chunk of Vincent's upper torso was ripped free. The sea filled immediately with a billowing plume of crimson blood; then the free-for-all began, dozens of the sharks darting in to claim their share.

The next attacker took his head off at the neck. Two others fought over his legs.

Mia watched in absolute horror as the cage continued to rise. Every instinct inside her screamed: *Go to him! Try and fight them off!*

194

Leonardo Feola had the knife ready.

He was holding it to the neck of the terrified eight-year-old girl while he waited for the drug mule in Seattle to give him the reassurance he needed.

He had already decided he was going to kill the girl anyway as soon as they had possession of the drugs. The girl Mariana had called his bluff in the most outrageous way. He would be losing face with his men if he backed down now.

Then came a tiny metallic noise from outside.

It sounded like a firearm being primed.

Leonardo frowned. Some gut instinct, some sixth sense deep inside him, seemed to recognize that the sound could be some sort of warning.

195

Mia could only watch in mute terror as her grandfather was rapidly dismembered.

He was already beyond help. And to move from the safety of the metal frame would have been suicide.

The speed. The aggression. It was an awesome display; nature at its most potent.

In as little as twenty seconds the sharks had eaten their fill. All that was left of Vincent Bascombe was the metal dive tank and a few shreds of torn neoprene. Even the watch had vanished.

Mia shrank back into the metal framework as the predators began to circle closer and closer.

How much air was left in the tank? She viewed the gauge through her tears.

Slowly, the frame continued to rise.

And the sharks readied for a new attack.

196

HIDA MOUNTAIN RANGE, JAPAN

The rat sniffed the air.

The creature raised itself on its back legs, recognizing the girl's voice as a familiar thing in this world of senseless destruction and pain.

Slowly, as if suspecting a trap, the rat moved forward towards her.

The creature nuzzled against her hand for a moment or two, then she picked it up and held it against her chest.

'Brad!' Saki's face broke into a smile of total ecstacy as she held her beloved pet in her arms.

The rat nestled against her, glad to be back where he belonged.

197

The window shattered.

The stun grenade hit the floor in the middle of the bar, the metal/oxidant mix of magnesium and ammonium perchlorate producing a blinding flash coupled with a deafening explosion.

Leonardo's men were incapacitated for precisely four seconds, the amount of time needed for the narcotics squad to rush the room.

A few shots were fired. One of Amadeu's men was hit in the shoulder. But the six men in the room were quickly overwhelmed as the SWAT team forced them to the floor at gunpoint.

The girl was found, curled up and whimpering with dread beneath a table.

Then, by the light of her high intensity torch, Amadeu saw Leonardo make it to a doorway at the back of the room.

She rushed after him, screaming at her men to follow.

198

The sharks were fighting to get at their prize.

Vincent's blood had sent them into a frenzy.

They were beating the bed frame with their snouts as they tried to pluck out the flesh within. From Mia's position it was a terrifying vision: all she could see was the open mouths of the sharks, the sharp rows of serrated teeth a blur of white amidst the confusion of sleek, twisting, bodies.

The predators were bending the bunk bed structure out of shape with the power of the assault.

Mia thought the frame must surely fail, that the metal would crack and splinter under the battering.

Still she kept rising through the water as the team above hauled—painfully slowly—on the rope.

Mia sucked desperately on the regulator.

The tank was out of air.

199

Mariana was still holding the mobile.

She was listening to the raid with her heart in her mouth.

She had the unit on speakerphone so that Cortes could listen in. They heard shouting, the thud of the stun grenade and the clatter of the handset falling to the floor as one of Leonardo's men screamed:

'I'll shoot her. I'll shoot her if you take one more . . .'

Then his voice was silenced by an unseen means.

Mariana stared in horror at the customs man as the sounds of the raid continued.

There were more shots. The agonized howl of a man in the background.

Had they already killed her sister?

'Ester?' she screamed into the handset. 'Ester, are you OK?'

200

HIDA MOUNTAIN RANGE, JAPAN

Professor Yamada decided on a new course of action. His intention was to find a first aid box so that at least he could help the wounded—and himself—to survive before assistance arrived.

He made it deeper into the carriages, noticing that the interior seemed to be closed off with some sort of plastic sheeting.

Strange.

He waited to catch his breath for a few moments and that was when he saw the butterfly—flying *inside* the wrecked carriage.

His mind churned as he realized what a strange coincidence this was: he'd never seen an Alpine Grayling in his life before; now he'd seen two in one day. Or maybe it was even the *same* butterfly. Now, that really would be something of note.

Then, to his amazement, the butterfly flew right up to him and landed on his hand.

Seeking him out. As if it had something to say.

201

Leonardo Feola shoved hard at the bathroom window.

He punched the frame clear out of the opening and scrambled clear of the sill as a brace of deafening explosions rang out behind him.

He landed on his side on hard compacted dirt. In an instant he was back on his feet and running. He could hear footsteps clattering behind him. The urgent shouts of the drug squad cops as they raced round the side of the building to intercept him.

He dived for the stairway, half running, half falling down the precipitous muddy steps. Then came a zigzag bend, he was moving like lightning, outstripping the cops through sheer speed and desperation.

Then he saw a high wall which looked familiar. The characteristic smell of pigs filled the night air. He recognized the place.

A perfect hiding place, if he could jump the wall.

202

MAYFIELD HOSPITAL, SEATTLE, USA

'Mari? Is that you?'

Mariana felt a hot trickle of teardrops cascade down her cheeks as she heard her sister's voice.

'It's me, are you OK? Please tell me you're all right.'

Mariana's sister sounded traumatized but she was at least alive.

'I'm all right, yes. I think . . .'

'Did you get hurt?' Mariana asked her.

'No. No. They haven't hurt me much. I just want to get home.'

'I'm so happy you're alive . . .' Mariana could hardly speak through the tears.

Then one of Amadeu's officers came on the line.

'We have to go now. Your sister is safe, we're going to get her home right away.'

And with that the call was cut.

203

Mariana turned to Cortes. Now that the trauma of the raid was over she could see the relief in his face.

She reached out and held his hand.

'Thank you,' she said, 'I appreciate what you've done.'

'That's OK.' Cortes looked touched by the gesture.

'Your friends did a good job too.'

'Yeah. We owe them one.'

A heartbeat later, the sound of gunfire erupted from the corridor outside.

'What the *hell*?' Cortes pulled his service revolver and took a quick look out of the door. 'Don't move from this room,' he told her.

Cortes stepped into the doorway to see what was happening.

Seven bullets punched into Nelson F. Muster's body as he reached for his mobile. The police marksmen were only reacting as they had been trained.

As far as they were concerned he could have been reaching for a weapon.

Two were head shots, instantly puncturing his skull and causing his neck to snap around as he was lifted clear off the floor. Five were shots to the body, causing so much trauma to his internal organs that he didn't even have time to draw another breath.

His mobile was silenced, blown into a thousand pieces by one of the rounds.

Nelson F. Muster was killed instantly.

The trainspotter's body fell twitching to the floor.

Leonardo Feola jumped the wall and landed in a heap of refuse, a semi-rotted pile of garbage and compost breaking his fall.

He could hear the cops running down the alley alongside.

Had they seen him jump into the yard?

The footsteps faded as the cops ran down the hill. The cries grew quieter.

They had missed him. By a hair's breadth he had clambered up the wall without being seen.

Leonardo felt a big smile break out as he congratulated himself. His entire team had been busted but the grand master was still free.

He waited until his breathing was under control. Then he rose from the pile of waste and walked over to the little shack in the corner of the yard.

He would hide there for the night, he decided, lie low for a while. Think about his next move.

Leonardo pulled back the corrugated iron sheet which served as a door and stepped into the darkness.

206

MAYFIELD HOSPITAL, SEATTLE, USA

'Projectile Number Eight' as the police investigation would later call it, did not hit Nelson F. Muster at all. It missed him by about two centimetres and ricocheted off the metallic shell of a fire extinguisher which was fixed to the wall of the corridor.

From there it flew down the corridor and hit Customs Inspector Cortes as he left the hospital ward room.

He took a single ricochet round to the side of the chest. The projectile hit one of his intercostal muscles and immediately 'fragged'. The metallic splinters (more than sixty of them) spun into the tissue of his lungs, heart, and liver.

Cortes tumbled, unconscious, to the floor.

Medics immediately rushed to his side, trying desperately to save his life.

207

Mia's eyes were bulging with oxygen deprivation.

Deadly carbon dioxide was building up in her blood to the point where her body would automatically trigger a reflex to breathe.

Her lungs were at the point of collapse.

She wanted nothing more than to open her mouth and scream with the agony of the moment.

The bunk bed frame was twisted and warped but the welds were still resisting.

The frame held—just, as the sharks turned on each other in frustration.

Moments later the bed frame was hauled out of the water and Mia was able to grab the biggest lungful of air she had ever taken. She took hold of a crew member's hand. More members of the family clutched at her, hauling her bodily out of the bed frame as the water around the scene exploded with thrashing sharks.

Mia fell onto the deck as the family and crew rushed to her aid.

208

The blinding muzzle flash of a handgun was the last thing that Leonardo Feola saw.

Two of Casio's bullets penetrated his upper body in fast succession, ripping his heart to shreds as a third round entered his head, splintering the skull and tearing a jagged track through his brain.

He fell, stone dead, onto the dirty floor of the shack.

209

MAYFIELD HOSPITAL, SEATTLE, USA

Mariana pulled the covers of the hospital bed over her head as the percussive retorts of the gunshots rang out.

Then she heard Cortes, crying out with pain for a few brief seconds. She *had* to see what was going on. She got out of the bed with some difficulty and limped to the doorway.

From her position, Mariana saw Cortes lying on the corridor floor as three police paramedics fought—and failed—to save his life. Her mind was completely unable to work it all out; *why* had he been shot? What was happening? In any case, no one seemed to be the least bit interested in *her*. Not a single one of the cops had spared her as much as a second glance.

Then, as Cortes's body was taken away, Mariana realized that his jacket was still hanging on the back of the door.

With her heart thrashing around in her chest, she reached into the inside pocket.

Her passport was still there. And her wallet with the open return ticket and the cash that the Rio cartel had given her to cover her time in Seattle.

This was it. She knew what she had to do.

210

Professor Yamada stared around at the bleak scene of tragedy which surrounded him, the catastrophic rail crash which had evidently cost many scores of lives. Everywhere he looked there was devastation and loss. It was chaos in its purest and most damaging form.

Chaos.

Could it be possible? Professor Yamada mused. A *connection* between the little brown butterfly and this mayhem?

Was it *all* connected?

He dismissed it from his mind. It was just too much to contemplate. Particularly for a scientist.

He shook his hand. 'Go away,' he told the creature, feeling a sudden revulsion for it.

His mind tried to snap back to the present. Ah yes. The first aid box. That was what he was seeking.

211

Mariana was shaky on her feet and her stomach hurt like hell after the procedure to remove the drug packages. But the pain was as nothing compared to the overwhelming urge to escape.

Her clothes had been put in a neat pile on a chair. She closed the door, took off the cotton hospital robe and dressed herself.

Then, her head held high, she made her way through the throng of police, medics, and crime scene photographers, and walked out of the hospital.

She made her way to a busy street and hailed a cab.

'Take me to the airport, please,' she told the driver.

'You on your way home?' the driver asked as he headed for Interstate 5.

'Yes,' Mariana told him.

'Had a good time here in Seattle?'

Mariana had no answer to that one.

212

HIDA MOUNTAIN RANGE, JAPAN

Professor Yamada reached the sealed off area. He figured there must be a first aid box inside. But he had to get this annoying plastic sheeting out of the way. He grabbed hold of the tape which was sticking the heavy duty plastic to the floor of the carriage and lifted it up with some difficulty.

Then he slid inside the kitchen area, not noticing that the butterfly followed him in.

He was overwhelmed by the gas in less than two seconds.

Rescuers wearing gas masks would later penetrate the sealed off kitchen area of the train where they found Yamada lying dead on the floor.

They couldn't help noticing an odd detail of the scene. A small brown butterfly had died in the same place. It was lying on the palm of the professor's outstretched hand.

Try as they might, the crash scene investigators never did work that one out.

About the author

Matt Dickinson is a writer and film maker with an enduring (and sometimes dangerous) passion for wild places and even wilder people. He was trained at the BBC and has subsequently filmed many award-winning documentaries for National Geographic television, Discovery Channel and Channel 4.

As a director/cameraman he has worked with some of the world's top climbers and adventurers, joining them on their expeditions to the Himalayas and beyond. Along the way he has survived some life-threatening dramas: an avalanche in Antarctica, a killer storm on Everest and a night-time 'grizzly bear' attack in the Yukon which wasn't quite what it seemed (actually they were beavers!).

Matt's proudest moment was filming on the summit of Mount Everest having successfully scaled the treacherous north face of the world's highest peak.

www.mortalchaos.com